The Princess of the Wind

Translated from Hungarian and with an Introduction by
Elizabeth Demeter

Illustrated by
Fruzsina Kun

Elek Benedek

The Princess of the Wind

Hungarian Fairy Tales

Corvina

Translated from *Magyar népmesék* (1954)
and *A vitéz szabólegény* (1959)

English translation © Elizabeth Demeter, 2014
Illustrations © Fruzsina Kun, 2014

Design by Sebastian Stachowski

Second printing, 2018

First published in Hungary 2014
by Corvina Books, Ltd.
1086 Budapest
Dankó utcat 4–8.
www.corvinakiado.hu

ISBN 978 963 13 6231 2

Contents

Introduction

Hungarian folk-tales are one of the world's most beautiful examples of oral storytelling. However, because of their language's isolation, they had been unknown in the English-speaking world yet. For me it could not have been a bigger aesthetic joy than selecting, translating and retelling these magical and original Hungarian tales. I grew up with them, my daughter grew up with them and I wish the young English readers could grow up with them as well. This collection of some thirty Hungarian folk-tales is filled with magic, cleverness and wit. The Hungarian zest for life and courage to tackle any obstacles, even the seven-headed dragon is evident in these wonderful tales.

The Carpathian basin was the cradle of these folk-tales. They have certain motives, which are so typical that we can say they represent the cultural 'subconscious' of the Hungarian people. For example 'the palace that stands on a duck's leg and goes around continuously', 'the seven-headed dragon', 'the witch whose nose reached her knees', 'the magic steed', 'the spring of eternal youth', 'the magically beautiful Miss Reed' and others have become a part of the Hungarian psyche and are well known to every Hungarian. Interestingly these motives are unknown in the Western European folklore.

Hungarian folk-tales had been transmitted by word of mouth for several centuries. There are many stories, which are connected with the famous Hungarian king Matthias Corvinus who lived in the 15th century. Many are full of earthly humour, cleverness and quick wit. The 'authors' of these stories were Hungarian peasants who gathered together in the evenings to husk corns or spin wool and to entertain themselves while they recounted stories, which they had heard from their parents and grandparents. They liberally embellished these tales and through them they transmitted cultural messages about themselves. Their tales absorbed and reflected the characters of the people who lived in the Carpathian basin for over a thousand years.

These Hungarian folk-tales were collected and written down for first time by Elek Benedek (1859–1929) or 'Uncle Benedek' as he was affectionately known in his native country. He emerged as Hungary's 'Brothers Grimm' as he travelled throughout Hungary/Transylvania and wrote down folk-tales and published them in the *Hungarian Popular Tales* (5 vols, 1894–96) in the 19th century. Before him through centuries-old storytelling tradition these tales only existed in aural form and were transmitted by word of mouth. Several generations grew up enjoying Elek Benedek's folk-tales, which became well known and popular throughout the land.

According to a Toscan proverb 'A folk-tale is not beautiful if nothing is added to it.' I also added my personal touch to each tale. However to keep their flavour intact in each case I kept the original story line and motives. I updated the tales from the dialects in which they were recorded by Elek Benedek. When a tale was lacking unity or freshness of authenticity I retold it. I enriched the tales' texts without altering their characters or unities. I touched up as delicately as possible those parts that were either missing or were too sketchy. I was careful not to alter the pristine freshness of the original story. I also made them linguistically up to date for today's English-speaking children.

These changes are my 'flowers' that I added to this 'bouquet' of thirty Hungarian folk-tales, which I kindly offer here to the young English-speaking readers.

Elizabeth Demeter

The Magically Beautiful Miss Reed

Once upon a time, beyond the seven seas and beyond even the glass mountain ranges, there lived a king who had two sons. When the king's eldest son grew into a man, he married a beautiful princess. The king tried to persuade his younger son to marry as well, but the young man replied that until he found the most beautiful princess in the whole world, he would not marry.

'You could be looking for a long time,' said his older brother, 'because I have married the most beautiful princess myself.'

'It is true that you have a most glorious wife,' answered the young prince, 'but I believe that somewhere there is a princess who is even more beautiful than your wife is.'

The younger son's old nurse overheard this conversation and when the older prince had gone away, she whispered to the young prince,

'In fact, there is a more beautiful princess in this world than your brother's wife. But your brother and his wife will never tell you that this magically beautiful Princess is her sister!'

'Really, good nurse? If that is true then I will go and find her.'

'Wait, my son,' said the old nurse, 'you cannot find her in her father's house.' The old nurse drew closer to the prince. 'Now listen carefully my boy, she is hidden away in a reed. Have you heard of the Black Sea? There are three reeds on the seventy-seventh island of the Black Sea and the magically beautiful Princess is in the middle reed and her two maidens are in the outer reeds. But there is such a heavy darkness on this island that you could hang your sword on it. An old witch guards the three reeds and she protects them better than she does her own eyes—he candle of her life would be extinguished if someone were to cut these three reeds.'

The prince did not need to be told twice, he leapt onto his fastest horse and rode away to find the magically beautiful Miss Reed. He travelled beyond the seven seas and by nightfall he reached a large dark forest. He found a small house in the forest and knocked on the front door. An old woman lived there, alone. The prince greeted her politely and she asked him, 'What are you doing here, my son, in this god-forsaken place?'

'I am looking for the magically beautiful Miss Reed who is hidden in a reed on the seventy-seventh island in the Black Sea. Have you heard of her?'

'I have not, nor any news from her, my sweet son.' The old woman reclined in her chair and then leaned forward again. 'But beyond the mountain in the round forest lives my sister and perhaps she knows something about your princess.' The old woman called out to her cat, 'Help this lad find his way!' and the cat seemed to understand.

It jumped out from the chimney corner and started walking onto the road. The prince followed it. By early dawn the cat and the prince had found the old woman's sister. The prince explained what had brought him there. The old woman listened and then thought for a while. She finally said,

'Oh, my son, never in your life will you reach that place unless you can find a magic steed who has drunk dragon milk, eaten embers from the glowing fire, and eaten the flames of fire.' The prince was startled. 'But, by Jove!' Exclaimed the old woman. 'What do I see on your head? Three golden hairs! What luck! During your voyage you will reach the top of a high mountain. Use these three golden hairs by striking them against a string—a magic steed will immediately appear in front of you.'

She gingerly plucked the three golden hairs from the prince's head and gave him a string. The prince thanked her very much and went on his way. He did not rest until he reached the top of the high mountain. Just as the woman had instructed, he struck the three golden hairs with the string and . . . wonder of wonders!! A fury of sound erupted from the sky and golden-haired stallions flew through the air and a beautiful magic steed glided out from among the golden-haired stallions. Flames burst forth from his huge nostrils. He neighed three times so that the whole world echoed and then gallantly presented himself before the prince.

'Here I am my master!' he said in a low rumble voice.

And can you imagine what happened to the string? It had become a beautiful golden bridle! It glittered and sparkled.

'Well my little master, I can ride fast like the wind, or faster like a bird or even as fast as a passing thought. How fast do you need to go?'

'Like a passing thought, my sweet horse!'

'Very well, my little master, I know your heart's desire. But before we go to the Black Sea's seventy-seventh island, we should go to the Sun's shining porch and get a flaming ray.'

The magic steed jumped in the air and flew as fast as a thought and in a twinkle the prince arrived at the gate of the earth. But there were two wolves at the gate, they were the guards and they said that they would not let the prince enter unless he gave them two pounds of horse flesh. 'Well,' thought the prince, 'I will not give them any flesh from my horse. I would rather give them some of my own.' And he took out his star-decked pen-knife and cut off two pounds of flesh from his thigh and threw it to the wolves.

'You may pass now,' they muttered.

The magic steed was once again flying through the air and the prince could not even blink or close his eyes when his horse said,

'Open your eyes, my little master, we have arrived at the shining porch of the Sun.'

The prince got off his horse and what a marvelous view he saw! There was a golden bath-tub with a fire-bath inside. He took a bath and then dried himself off with a golden towel that was on a diamond pin. He used a golden comb on a silver shelf to comb his hair. There was a big mirror in which he looked at himself. But listen to what happened next!

An angry old man, certainly a servant of the Sun, came to the porch. He saw the prince as he was looking at himself in the mirror. Very angrily he blew at him and his breath turned into a huge tornado. The whirling wind carried away the prince and his horse for seventy-seven thousand miles and even then their feet could not reach the earth. Finally, they fell down into a black hole and could not see the sky or the earth.

Oh, the prince became very sad! He thought that he would not see the blessed shining sun ever again if he could not bring one of its flaming rays back to the Black sea's seventy-seventh island. He and his horse crawled on their knees, inching forward; sometimes stepping on snakes and frogs and when seven days and seven nights passed they reached a big iron gate. It was not worth crawling on their knees to this point since a hundred-headed dragon was guarding the iron gate. And he would not let the prince go through the gate! That was for sure!

The poor prince felt hopeless and was thinking of a way out as he was fumbling in the dark when he suddenly found a little stick. But is wasn't a stick at all, it was a flute! As the prince was very sad he tried to comfort himself by blowing into the flute; it sounded as beautiful as if it were the music of angels. And what do you think happened next? The hundred-headed dragon lay down on the earth and did not move at all not even one of his heads as he was listening the sound of the flute. And the prince found his courage and passed through the iron gate.

At that moment as he passed through the gate the darkness started to fade away and who do you think he saw? A beautiful girl stood before him. She was Dawn herself, the kindest and most cherished daughter of the Sun. Dawn smiled at the prince and let him sit on her winged horse and she took him far away. First she took him to the bronze forest where the sun's loggers were working. They chopped the trees down, cut them up, put them on their carts and took them to the Sun's kitchen. Next, Dawn took the prince to the silver forest where silver birds were singing beautiful songs and the silver trees bowed in front of Dawn three times. From here Dawn took the prince to the golden forest. The forest came alive with the songs of the golden birds and again the golden trees bowed three times in front of Dawn.

In the middle of this golden forest was Dawn's garden and in the middle of this garden was her diamond palace. As soon as Dawn arrived, the sparkling stars came together and when she waved her hand a coach made from clouds descended from the air. There was a golden seat in this coach for the prince and Dawn to sit. They flew higher and higher until they reached the porch of the shining Sun. Here Dawn selected a flaming ray and she spun it into the prince's hair and said,

'Now you can go my prince and you will find the Magically Beautiful Miss Reed.' And in that moment—who knows from where—the prince's magic steed suddenly appeared before them. The prince got on its back and it began to gallop towards the Black Sea. All of a sudden the steed said,

'Listen, my little master, soon I will take you to the seventy seventh island in the Black Sea. I must warn you to be very careful when you cut down the three reeds. You must cut them down all at once or your life will be over. Remember not to split the three reeds before you get some water! If you don't have some water to give the girls who are inside the reeds, they will die the moment that you rescue them!'

The steed galloped for seven days and seven nights until he reached the seventy seventh island in the Black Sea. This island was so dark that the prince could have hung his sword on it. But he took off his hat and the flaming ray that was spun into his hair blazed up and suddenly the whole island became bright. Indeed, there were the three reeds—in the middle of the island. As soon as the prince walked towards them, they bowed in front of him, even though the air was breezeless. The prince pulled out his sword, swung it over his head and with one swift stroke he cut down the three reeds at their roots. And, believe it or not, black blood bubbled from the roots, and wailing could be heard from the depths of the earth. That black blood was the old witch's blood and it was she who was wailing. The prince took the three reeds in his lap and said to his horse,

'Now my dear horse, take me home, it has been a long time since I have seen my mother and father.'

While the magic steed galloped, the prince looked at the three reeds and he ached to cut into them to see if it was true, that girls were inside them. It was possible that someone was fooling him, he thought, and that he had come in vain to the Black Sea's seventy-seventh island. With his star-decked pen-knife he cut open one of the reeds. Suddenly a very beautiful girl fell from its folds. She was one of the maids of the magically beautiful Miss Reed.

'Give me water quickly, or I am going to die.'

The prince became alarmed. He would have given her water but he did not have any. He did not even blink once and the girl died. He could hear a loud cry from the two other reeds as the two other girls wept for their friend. The poor prince became very sad. He tried to revive the girl, but in vain. He dismounted his horse, dug a grave and buried her.

The prince continued to ride further and, God knows why, but he cut the second reed too. And the same thing happened as before. He could not give water to the girl and the second maid of the magically beautiful Miss Reed died as well. Now the prince pledged to himself that he would guard the third reed as if his life depended upon it. He would not cut the third reed until he had reached a spring. But he so craved to see the magically beautiful Miss Reed! The place which he passed through was a desert and he could not see any water anywhere. Just as he felt that he would die of thirst, the magic steed came down from the air to land beside a bubbling spring.

'Now, my dear master, you can cut the reed after you have drawn some water into your hat.'

The prince did so and then he tenderly cut the reed. He was very careful not to harm the delicate body of the magically beautiful Miss Reed. As he did, what do you think happened next? A most beautiful girl stepped out from the reed. She was as dazzling as the Sun! Nobody had seen such a lovely girl before. She and the prince fell into each other's arms.

'You are mine and I am yours till death do us part!'

And they both mounted the magic steed. The horse flew through the air and he came down in the court of the prince's father. The king was sitting there with his older son and his daughter-in-law and they were very surprised. They cried their eyes out for the younger prince as they did not know where he was and did not think that they were going to see him again. And there he was. And he also brought with him the most beautiful princess in the world! The old king was very glad and his son and daughter-in-law were happy too.

A splendid wedding was held that very day with great happiness and merry-making and they both lived happily ever after for many, many years.

The Golden Tulip

Once upon a time, a very long time ago, far beyond the end of the world there lived a king. The king had a son and when he grew up, he said to his father, 'Your Majesty, my beloved father, I have made up my mind. I am going away and will not stop until I find the most beautiful princess have to marry.'

'It is fine with me, my dear son,' said the king, 'I wish you good luck on your voyage!'

And the prince went on his way. He travelled through dark woods and open fields when he finally arrived at a very dense forest. He was riding on his horse when he saw a little fish in a puddle of water. The fish was suffocating and struggling for it's life and when it saw the prince, the fish asked, 'Please good prince, help me. Take me to the river or I will die in this puddle.'

The prince picked up the little fish and took it to the river. There the fish said, 'Thank you for your kindness, young prince. Please take off one of my scales and keep it with you. Make sure you guard it very carefully. If you ever find yourself in trouble, just throw it into a river and I will be right there to help you.'

The prince took one of the scales then threw the little fish into the river and continued on his way. He soon reached another dense forest and there he saw a crow trapped a tree branch. The crow's legs were stuck in the branch and he could not free himself. When the crow saw the prince, it asked, 'Please free me from my trap, good master, and you will not be sorry.'

The prince climbed up the tree and freed the crow. With his beak the crow pulled out one of it's feathers and gave it to the prince then said, 'One good turn deserves another. If you ever find yourself in trouble just shake my feather and I will be there right away to help you.'

The prince said good-bye to the crow then resumed his journey. All of a sudden he saw a gray-haired old man standing beside a spring who wanted to drink some water but was unable to bend down. He asked the prince', 'Please help me, my son, I am dying of thirst but I cannot reach the water.'

The prince immediately took off his hat, filled it with water and gave it to the old man.

'Thank you, my son, you saved my life. I give you two strands of my hair. If you ever find yourself in trouble throw these strands of hair in the air and they will find me. I will come to help you even from the end of the world'.

The prince took the two strands of hair and thanked him for his offer and said good bye. He resumed his journey and soon he arrived at a big city. He was surprised to see that the houses in the city were all covered by black canvas. He met a man on the street whose beard reached his knees and he asked him, 'Tell me, my good man, why is this city in mourning and why are all the houses covered in black canvas?'

'Oh, my son, there is a good reason. Our king has a daughter whose beauty made her world-famous. She decided she was only going to marry a young man who was able to hide from her so cleverly that she could not find him. According to her wish every candidate would be allowed to have three trials. If she finds him on the first try or the second try he can still live, but if she finds him the third time, he loses his head. Up to this time ninety-nine young men have tried their luck and ninety-nine young men have lost their heads. This is the reason our city is in mourning. If you try your luck, my son, you will be the one hundredth victim.'

The prince said, 'If the girl is really as beautiful as you say I will try my luck.'

At that moment a coach was heading towards them. It was pulled by six horses. Inside the coach the prince saw such a breathtakingly beautiful girl that he could not believe his eyes. He had never seen such beauty in his life, not even in his dreams.

The prince asked the man, 'Who is this girl, good man?'

'This is our princess.'

The prince became very excited. He went directly to the king's palace and said to the king, 'Your Majesty, I heard about the ninety-nine young men who tried their luck. I too, would like to try mine.'

'My son, the king said, 'I am sorry for you as you look a fine young man. But I cannot change my daughter's wish. She is my only child. Try your luck, hide yourself if you can but be careful not to let her to find you.'

While they were talking the princess arrived home. She came into the room and when she saw the prince she told him, 'It will be better for you prince, if you don't try your luck. Go home before you lose your head.'

'I shall take my chance,' the prince said, 'I cannot live without you.'

So the prince went out of the palace. He soon became very despondent as he did not know where to hide. He walked throughout the city, went to the forest and tried to find a place to hide so the princess could not find him. Suddenly he remembered the little fish—maybe it could help him. He went to the near-by river, took out the scale and threw it into the river, and what do you think happened? The little fish appeared immediately and asked the prince, 'What is the trouble, my good prince?'

And the prince explained everything to the little fish.

'Oh, don't be afraid,' the little fish said, 'I will call the river's biggest fish and he will swallow you. I am sure the princess won't find you there.'

And the little fish disappeared for a short time and when it came back a huge fish was swimming after him. The huge fish opened his mouth, which was as big as a house, the prince jumped into it and the big fish swallowed him.

Meanwhile the princess started to look for the prince. She looked for him everywhere and spent half the day searching. When she walked to the river-side she suddenly ordered the royal fishermen to catch the biggest fish from the river. She found out that the prince was hiding in his stomach. When her servants caught the biggest fish and pulled him to shore, they cut the fish's stomach open and the prince jumped out.

So you see, the prince failed in his first trial but he did not give up hope and decided to hide from the princess for a second time.

He went into the forest and decided that he would ask the crow for help. He shook the feather which the crow gave him and in a second the crow appeared in front of him and asked the prince, 'What is your problem, my master?'

The prince told him what happened. The crow started to caw and in a minute the sky turned black as hundreds of crows flew towards them from every direction. They asked the crow and the prince, 'What's wrong? What's wrong?'

'Do any of you know a good hiding place?' asked the crow.

'Of course we know,' cawed the crows.

All the crows flew through the forest while the prince followed close behind. They took the prince to a tall mountain whose top almost reached the sky. There was a deep pit at the top of the mountain and they asked him to hide there. But it was all for naught, as the princess found him the very next day.

Now the poor prince became very scared and sad. He knew he could easily lose his head, nevertheless he decided he would try to hide from the princess a third time. He remembered the old man's two strands of hair. He took them out and threw them into the wind.

The old man came in a second and asked, 'What is your trouble, my son?'

'Oh, I have a big problem, good man. Unless I can find a perfect hiding spot where no one can discover me, I will lose my head.'

'Is that all? I can easily help you. Who do you have to hide from?'

'From the princess, good man.'

'I see. I will show you how you can be in plain sight of her and still she won't see you.'

The old man grabbed the prince's neck, twisted it once and at that moment the prince became a golden tulip. The old man then put the golden tulip on his hat and went into the city. The princess was walking towards him as she was on her way looking for the prince. She saw the wonderful golden tulip and asked the old man, 'Oh, what a beautiful tulip! Can I have it?'

'I am sorry but I cannot give it to you,' answered the old man.

'If you let me have it I will give you so much gold that you and your family will be rich for the rest of your lives.'

'I beg you, my princess forgive me, but I cannot give it to you for all the treasures in the world.'

And the princess realized that she could not have the golden tulip. She was disappointed but could waste no more time with the old man as she had to look for the prince! She tried but could not find him anywhere on the first day and not on the second day and not even on the third day. Finally at the end of the third day the king announced that the prince could come out now from his hiding place as he won the princess' hand.

The old man heard about the news, twisted the golden tulip once and the prince re-appeared right in front of him. You can imagine how overjoyed and happy the prince was! He ran into the palace, knelt down in front of the princess and said,

'I am yours and you are mine, till death do us apart!'

They held a magnificent wedding that very day. After the wedding the young couple went to visit the prince's family and there they had another feast. They may be dancing even now.

The Spring of Eternal Youth

Once upon a time there lived an old king who had three handsome sons. Even though he seemed to have everything he could want the king was not completely happy and so he would smile with one eye but cry with the other. And nobody knew the reason for this. Nobody had ever asked. One day the three princes decided to find out why one of his eyes was crying. First the eldest went to the king's room, greeted his father politely, and sat down.

'Your Majesty, my dear father, all three of your sons are worried about you. Please tell me, what is the reason that one of your eyes is smiling and the other is crying?'

But the king became furious! He didn't say a word, he picked up a knife from the table and threw it at his son! Luckily it did not reach his eldest son but struck the wall behind him. Shocked, the prince ran from the room into the courtyard. His younger brothers asked him,

'What did our father say?'

The boy caught his breath, 'Go inside and you will find out.'

So the middle prince went to his father and the very same thing happened to him. He also ran out to the courtyard but he also did not tell the youngest prince what happened to him. It was now the youngest brother's turn. He went to the king's room, stood beside the door and asked his father,

'Tell me, my dear father why is one of your eyes crying and the other one smiling?'

The king held a huge club in his hand which he threw with all his might towards his youngest son! Had it hit him he would have perished on the spot. The club thudded against the wall and the youngest prince picked it up and took it to his father.

'Here is the club, my father you can kill me now if this is your wish.'

The king's mood changed instantly. He calmed down and said to his son,

'I can see, my dear son that you are not afraid of your own shadow. You should know that one of my eyes is smiling because I love to see you and your brothers. The other one is crying because I am an old man and I could die any time. If I should take a sip of the water of spring of eternal youth then both of my eyes would be smiling!'

'If that will make you happy, dear father, I will seek the water of spring of eternal youth.' The young man turned from his father's room and went to the courtyard to tell his brothers what troubled their father. They decided to go in different directions and not rest until they found the spring of eternal youth. From the stable the older princes found two beautiful horses for themselves but the youngest could not make up his mind. While he was looking around a very lean filly stroked his face lightly with his tail,

'Listen, little master, if you would like luck to be on your side, choose me.'

And so the youngest prince did not hesitate, he chose the lean filly right then. His two older brothers laughed at him when they saw his filly. 'Will the horse carry you, or will you carry the horse?!' They almost fell over they were laughing so hard. Finally they jumped on their horses and rode away as fast as the wind. The youngest prince could still hear their far-away chuckles floating over the horizon.

The lean filly staggered out of the courtyard and reeled onto the streets. At the edge of the city the horse asked the youngest prince,

'Why are you sad my young master?'

'I am sad,' the prince said, 'because my brothers have already reached the end of the world and I will never catch up with them.'

'Don't be sad, my dear master, you are not only going to catch up but you will out-run them. Your two brothers will stop at the first tavern and play cards with twelve men who are bandits in disguises. The disguised bandits will take all their money, horses and clothes. And they will have to stay in the inn as servants and work off their debts.'

As the filly said these words he shook himself, and wonder of wonders, in a twinkle of an eye he turned into a wonderful steed with six legs!

'Jump on my back, my master and tell me. How fast would you like to go? Like the wind or a bird or even faster—as fast as a passing thought?'

'It's up to you,' the youngest prince said, 'as long as we find the spring of eternal youth.'

And the steed jumped in the air and flew as fast as a passing thought or maybe even faster. In a second they arrived at a thick forest and the steed touched down in front of a little house. Inside the prince found an old woman whose nose was so long that it reached her knees.

'Good evening, old lady.'

'You can thank your luck that you called me 'old lady'. What are you up to?' she asked raising her eyebrows and rubbing her nose.

And the youngest prince told her that he was looking for the spring of eternal youth.

'I have heard about that spring,' the old woman said, 'although I cannot tell you where you can find it. See that high mountain? On the other side at the bottom lives

my sister. Perhaps she knows more about that than me. If you ever find the spring of eternal youth, my son, please bring me a jug of it. I would make it worth your while. Here is a golden brush, maybe you will find some use for it one day.'

The youngest prince accepted the brush and thanked the old woman. On his way out he grabbed a jug and jumped on his steed. The steed flew over the high mountain and arrived at the little house. The prince went inside and found an even older woman there. He greeted her politely,

'Good day, old lady.'

'You can thank your luck that you called me 'old lady.' What are you up to?' And the prince told her what he was looking for.

'I heard about that spring,' the old woman said 'and I would also like a jug of that. But unfortunately I cannot tell you where you could find it. But do you see that high mountain? My sister lives at the bottom of the other side and she knows everything. She'll be able to help you. Take this golden towel, my son perhaps it will be useful. But do not forget me! Please bring me a jug of water of the spring of eternal youth on your way home!'

And the prince picked up another jug and continued his journey. His steed flew over the high mountain and in a second he was in front of the third woman's house. The prince went inside, greeted the old woman who was about a thousand years old and told her the reason of his journey.

'You are lucky, my son,' the old woman said. 'I can help you. You can find the spring of eternal youth in the palace of Ilona, queen of the fairies. See this high mountain in front of us? If you fly over it, you reach the Blue Sea. There are seventy seven islands in the Blue Sea and the queen's castle is on the seventy seventh one. Her palace stands on a golden duck's leg and it turns around and around continuously. If you want to get inside your horse must jump over the castle's wall into the courtyard. But be very careful. You will have to braid your horse's tail. If even one single hair touches the castle's wall, the palace would sound an alarm and the fairies would wake up and capture you. But if you don't make any noise and you're able to get inside, you will find the Fairy queen's bedroom in the middle of the castle. Her bed is floating between the sky and the ground, and a flower-staircase leans against her bed. Above her bed there is a golden cage with a golden finch. Tie the beak of the finch with a single golden hair otherwise its singing will wake up the Fairy queen. A spring flows at each of the two corners of her room. One is the water of death and the other is the water of eternal youth. Draw water from both of them and, my dear son, I beg you, bring me a jug of the water of the spring of eternal youth. I would like to be young again.'

In addition to this advice the old woman also gave the prince a golden bridle as a present. The prince thanked her warmly for her good advice and her present and said good-bye. He soon reached the Fairy queen's palace and jumped over its wall. Not a living soul noticed him or his horse. He went into the queen's bedroom and indeed her bed was floating between the ground and the sky. He went up on the flower-staircase and found the Fairy queen sleeping in her bed. Her whole body was covered by her long golden hair. The prince looked at the beautiful Fairy queen and he fell in love with her at once. He wished he could take her with him but he had to remind himself that he did not come here for Ilona but for the water of spring of eternal youth! So, as he was told, he quickly tied up the finch's beak with a single golden hair and drew a jug of water from the spring of eternal youth and a jug of water from the spring of death. He also drew three jugs of water from the spring of eternal youth for the three old women. After leaving the queen's room he leapt onto his steed but in his hurry he forgot to properly braid his horse's tail. As the horse flew over the castle's wall one single hair brushed against it. The palace thundered loudly and the fairies all woke up. They realized what was happening and angrily ran after the prince. The steed flew as fast as a thought but suddenly said,

'Look back, my little master what do you see? I can sense trouble with my right ear.'

The prince looked back and said,

'Oh my God! We are in a big trouble, my dear horse. The fairies are after us.'

'Do not be afraid, just throw the golden brush back towards them.' The prince threw back the golden brush and its bristles grew into tall trees and soon a thick forest made it very difficult for the fairies to pass through. After a few minutes the steed said,

'Look back, my dear master and tell me what do you see now? I can sense trouble with my left ear.'

'We have the same trouble, my sweet horse. The fairies are catching up to us and will capture us.'

'Do not be afraid, my little master just throw back the golden towel.'

And the prince threw back the golden towel and wonder of wonders! It turned into an ocean and the fairies could not cross it without wasting time. The steed flew as fast as he could but after a while he again said,

'Look back, my master I can sense trouble with both of my ears.'

The prince looked back and said,

'This time we do not have any chance whatsoever. The fairies will reach your tail in a few seconds.'

'Do not be scared, my master just throw back the golden bridle.'

And the prince threw back the golden bridle and it turned into a rain of fire. To save their lives the fairies had to turn back. And so they did although they were furious that they had to go home empty handed.

So you see, the prince and his horse finally managed to escape from the fairies. On his way back the prince decided to visit the three old women. He gave a jug of water of spring of eternal youth to each one of them. They only had a sip of it and they turned into young girls again. You cannot imagine how happy they were!

And the youngest prince continued his journey and arrived at the inn where his two brothers had lost their money, their horses and their every possession. They were still at the inn working off their debt. The youngest prince paid the owner everything they owed and the three of them departed together.

During their voyage home the youngest prince explained to his brothers how lucky he was. He had both the water of death and the water of spring of eternal youth! But his two older brothers became jealous and envious of their younger brother and they decided to get rid of him. At night fall as their brother slept they tied up his hands and legs and threw him into a deep pit. Then they departed for their city and they took with them the water of spring of eternal youth and the water of death. When they arrived at the castle they boasted loudly to their father of their many heroic deeds. They said they travelled the whole world to fulfill his wish.

But their boast was all in vain as one of the king's eyes continued to cry. He cried because his youngest son had not come home and he was worried about him. Furthermore, his two older sons, with all their boasting, could not tell him which jug contained the water of spring of eternal youth and which contained the water of death.

And what do you think happened to the youngest prince? The next morning his steed found him sitting in the bottom of the pit. He lowered his tail to the young prince who was able to grab it even though his hands were still tied. And his steed pulled him up out of the pit! The prince rode home but before he reached the palace he dressed up as if he was a servant. When he saw the king he asked him to hire him as a coachman. The king did not recognize the young prince in his servant's clothes but he liked the handsome young man and decided to hire him as his coachman.

Time went by and the old king still did not know which jug contained the water of death and which had the water of spring of eternal youth. He proclaimed throughout the whole country that he was going to give six cartful of gold to any person who could tell him which was which.

Fortune hunters came from every corner of his country and they tried their luck but none of them could tell the king which one was the water of death and which one was the water of spring of eternal youth. Finally the newly hired coachman came along and told the king which jug had the water of spring of eternal youth and the water of death. And the old king immediately drank from the water of spring of eternal youth and... wonder of wonders! Right away he turned into a young handsome man looking very much like his own sons.

The king was overjoyed but his happiness did not last long. One day news reached him that Ilona, queen of the fairies, had started out with all her soldiers and she had a golden bridge built between her palace and the king's castle. She was determined to walk into the castle on that bridge and have everyone killed if the king will not give up the son who had taken a jug of water of the spring of eternal youth and a jug of water of death from her. So the king told his oldest son,

'Go my son, if you really were there and ask for the fairies' queen's forgiveness.'

The eldest prince was scared but he had to go. He did not even dare to step on the golden bridge, he just walked beside it and stood with downcast eyes in front of the Fairy queen. And the queen asked him,

'Is it true, prince that you were in my palace?'

'Yes it was me.' answered the eldest prince.

'If you were there, tell me on what does my palace stand?'

'Just like the others—on the ground.'

'And where are my springs of the water of eternal life and death?'

'Just like the other springs, in the earth.'

'And where is my bed?'

'Just like every other bed—on the ground.'

'You are a liar, nothing you told me is true. You were not in my palace. Tell your father to send me the son who was really in my palace.'

And the eldest prince went back to the castle, feeling ashamed. Now the king sent his middle son to the fairies' queen but he met an even worse fate than his brother. The Fairy queen became so mad at him for his lies that she had him whipped fifty times. And the middle prince went home hurt and humiliated. The king was puzzled, he did not know what to do. Now both of his eyes were crying.

Then his new coachman visited him a little later and said,

'I put my life in your hands, Your Majesty. I am sorry to see how unhappy you are. Perhaps I can help you.'

'You cannot help me, my dear coachman. I have a hopeless problem. I wish my youngest son were at home! I would not be sad anymore.'

And the 'coachman' said,

'Your Majesty, let me have the golden velvet clothing that your youngest son used to wear.'

'Very well,' the king said and he gave it to him. The prince put it on and the king immediately recognized him. He shouted joyfully,

'You are my dear son!'

And the youngest prince took his leave at once and departed to see the Fairy queen. He jumped on his steed and rode to the middle of the golden bridge where the queen was waiting. When she saw him she thought to herself, 'Now this could be the real one! I believe he was the one and nobody else in my palace'. As she thought about it, the prince stood in front of her and saluted,

'I am here, Your Majesty, and I was in your palace.'

'If you were there, tell me on what does my palace stand?'

'Your palace, Your Majesty stands on a golden duck's leg on the seventy seventh island of the Blue Sea and it turns around continuously.'

'That is right. You are telling the truth. Now tell me, where are my springs of the water of eternal life and death?'

'Your springs are in your bedroom at the two corners. One is the source of eternal youth and the other is the water of death.'

'You are right again.'

'And where is my bed?'

'Your bed, Your Majesty, is floating between the ground and the sky and one can climb up to it on a flower-staircase.'

'You were in my palace, you are the one!' shouted the Fairy queen.' And I am yours and you are mine from now on.' Both the Fairy queen and the prince threw their arms wide open and hugged each other happily.

To everyone's surprise the threat of war had turned into a wedding feast! Everyone was overjoyed and now both of the king's eyes were laughing. And he gave his kingdom to his youngest son and they lived there happily ever after.

Matthew the Goose Boy

Once upon a time, there lived a poor woman who had a teenaged son, Matthew the goose boy. His only duty was to look after his mother's geese. One day she said to him,

'Go, my son, to the city of Dobrog, where there is an annual fair. Take sixteen of our finest geese with you and sell them all. But don't sell a pair for less than two silver pieces or I will punish you.'

So Matthew took the sixteen geese to the city fair of Dobrog. When the landlord of the city saw the lovely geese he approached Matthew,

'How much do you want for a pair of your geese, poor lad?'

'Two silver pieces,' answered Matthew.

"What? Two silver pieces? One is more than enough.'

'No, not enough,' said Matthew. 'I would not sell them even to the king for under two silver pieces.'

'Really?' The man's eyes narrowed into little black slits, 'You will see that I will give you two silver pieces then, guaranteed.'

The landlord made a sign to his servants and they took the sixteen geese and Matthew with them. And the landlord had Matthew whipped twenty five times in his courtyard instead of giving him two silver pieces.

'You can go home now,' said the landlord.

'And how about my money?' screamed Matthew.

'Oh! You want more? Whip him again!' The landlord ordered his servants.

And the servants whipped Matthew again twenty five times. He finally staggered out of the landlord's courtyard in a terrific pain. But before he left he turned back and, standing at his full height, he said,

'Remember, sir that I will beat you three times for your treatment.'

The landlord laughed heartily and did not take Matthew's threat seriously. Years passed and Matthew grew into a handsome young man. He caught word that the landlord was building a castle for himself. He fancied himself a king! Matthew dressed himself in sophisticated carpenter's clothes and went into the city to find the landlord's courtyard.

When he arrived he began to measure and scrutinize the rafters and all the while he was shaking his head. The landlord noticed him and asked,

26

'Sir, what are you inspecting my rafters for?'

'Well, I am a famous foreign carpenter,' said Matthew 'I've travelled through many countries and I've seen many castles being built and I can tell you that these rafters are not good enough for your castle. You'll need a better quality wood.'

The landlord looked a little surprised, and he said, 'That is not a problem, I have many beautiful trees in my forest and we can choose the most suitable ones to build better rafters. He immediately ordered a hundred men with axes to go to the forest and asked Matthew to accompany him in his coach.

So the landlord and Matthew went to the forest. Matthew showed the landlord which trees he should have chosen for his castle. And the hundred men with axes began to cut down the trees.

'My lord, these are good logs but I still cannot see the one you need the most,' said Matthew. 'Let's go further.'

So Matthew and the landlord went deeper into the forest and when they could no longer hear the noise of the servants' axes, Matthew stood in front of a huge tree and began to examine it. He even hugged it with his arms and smelled its bark!

'Well, I believe this one will be a good one,' he said. 'Please come here, my lord. If you hug this tree yourself, I think you'll see what I mean.'

And what do you think happened next?

As soon as the landlords' arms were around the enormous tree, Matthew quickly fastened his hands with a string at the other side of the tree and grabbed a big cudgel. And he whipped the landlord's back fifty times! When he counted the fiftieth whips he laughed at him and said,

'I am not a carpenter, sir I am Mathew the Goose Boy! Do you remember my promise? I will still beat you two more times!'

Then he left the landlord and disappeared in the forest. The servants did not find their master until the evening. He became seriously ill as a result of the beating and none of his doctors could cure him. He announced everywhere that he would welcome any famous doctor into his house. Matthew heard this announcement and dressed himself like a doctor. He went to the manor house where he introduced himself to the servants as a foreign 'miracle' doctor who could cure the landlord. The servants were happy to see him and they immediately swept him upstairs to their master's chamber.

Matthew bowed before the sickly man. 'I can cure you sir, in just one day,' he said. 'Please send all of your servants to the forest to look for a special herb. And the rest is my business.'

You can imagine how quickly the landlord sent all of his servants to the forest to find the mysterious herb and he not only sent his servants but all of the servants' children too. Nobody stayed at the house.

And Matthew was waiting exactly for this! He picked up a cane and whipped the landlord's backside with it.

'I am not a miracle doctor, sir.' he said. 'My name is Mathew the Goose Boy. Do you remember my promise? Another beating still will come. Don't worry: I am going to pay you my debt back in full.'

Some time passed by, one year or maybe two years and Matthew never set his feet in the city. But when people already started to forget about him, he dressed up as a horse-trader and went to the horse fair in the city of Dobrog. He walked up and down at the fair and listened to people's negotiations. He also stopped in front of some horses and bargained over them. Suddenly he heard about a man who had two beautiful horses but could not sell them because they were coughing.

He approached the man and told him,

'Hello, my good man! I will buy your horses, but only on one condition. When the landlord of Dobrog comes to the horse-fair you will shout to him,

'I am Matthew the Goose Boy!'

'If this is your wish I can do that very easily,' said the man. They had a deal and Matthew bought the man's horses. The fair was almost over when the landlord arrived sitting in his coach.

Matthew said to the man, 'The landlord is coming. Now shout to him, 'I am Matthew the Goose Boy' then run away as quickly as you can.'

The man stood in front of the coach and shouted out loud,

'I AM MATTHEW THE GOOSE BOY!' and he ran away as fast as his legs would go.

'Quickly, quickly,' the landlord ordered his servants, 'un-harness the horses, ride them, go after that rascal and bring him back to me!'

While the servants rode away on the horses to catch the man, Matthew suddenly appeared beside the coach where the landlord was alone. And he beat him for a third time. When he had finished, he began to run away but suddenly he turned back and shouted to the landlord,

'I am the real Matthew the Goose Boy and not that man! I kept my promise did I not? I beat you three times for my geese.'

And this is the end of my tale. If Matthew had beaten the landlord one more time, my tale would have been even longer.

Elizabeth the Fairy

Once upon a time, there lived a poor man with his wife and they had three sons. They were as poor as a family of church mice. Sometimes the poor man and his family could not eat as they rarely ever had even dry bread in their cupboards. One day the eldest son said,

'Father, I don't want to sit at home and always be hungry, I would rather go away and look for work.'

'Very well', said the poor man, 'then go and may God be with you'. The boy's mother baked cookies for him and the young lad left his home and made his way down the path and through a deep forest. He came across an old man. 'Good day, sir.'

'Good day, my son. Where are you going in the woods as dark as these?'

'I am looking for work, sir and am hopeful that I can find something to do.'

'Well then, this is your lucky day, my son,' said the old man with a chortle, 'as I am looking for a servant.' And the old man continued, 'If you stay with me, in three days a whole year will have passed, and if you work very hard I will give you a bit of land and a bushel of wheat and if you plough the field with my oxen and sow the wheat, then you can keep the harvest.'

The young man accepted the offer and the old man's eyes twinkled.

The next morning the lad rose early and made his way to the field. As he approached it he could see that the land was covered with thorny bushes! He said to himself, 'By the time I finish clearing these bushes my beard will have grown to my knees! He left the oxen behind and returned to his parents house.

Surprised to see their brother back so soon, the younger boys asked, 'Where have you been? What happened to you?'

'You will find out if you go away, just like I did.' Said the lad earnestly.

So, on the next day the middle brother followed the same path as his older brother. He also met the old man and became his servant. But as soon as he went to the field he saw the thorny bushes, he too was discouraged and left the oxen behind and returned to his parents' house.

His younger brother asked him,

'Where have you been my brother, what happened to you?'

'Go away my little brother, as we did, and you will see.'

So the youngest lad followed the well-trodden path into the deep dark woods as his brothers had. He met the old man with the twinkle in his eye and he agreed to work as his servant. The old man offered him a bushel of wheat to sow, and if he worked through the whole year, which for him lasted three days, he could keep the harvest.

The youngest brother tripped along the path towards the field with the master's dog following along behind. But when he saw the field was covered with thorny bushes he did not hesitate a moment. He swung his axe high and began to chop the bushes, which the dog placed into a neat pile. By the time the sun had set the young man had cut down all the bushes and had ploughed a large section of the field too. As soon as he had served his three days, the master said, 'Now, my son, you have certainly worked diligently during the year and so I will grant you next year's harvest.'

The youngest son thanked him and promptly returned to his parents' house.

Everybody was curious. 'What did you do? Where have you been for the last year?'

He only said, 'Next summer will reveal where I have been and what I have done.'

But the three boys' mother and father were upset and felt disappointed with their three sons as none of them had brought home food and they were going to die from hunger!

The youngest son kept his secret well until summer arrived and the time for reaping the harvest had come. When the time was right he announced, 'Father, last year I worked for an old man and sowed a bushel of wheat. Let's go reap the harvest which he owes me for my hard work!'

The poor man, his wife and their three sons all went to the field where the youngest son had sowed the wheat and Wonder of wonders! The field was covered with pure golden wheat so bright that they had to shade their eyes. You can imagine how happy they were! The poor man said, 'Now my sons, I will go home with your mother, hire wagons and we will be back soon. Until we return protect the wheat and watch for burglars.'

The boys were very careful not to let the sparrows pick even one single grain from the stalks. But through their squinting eyes they could see a woodpecker fly down and swiftly pick off an ear of wheat and hush....fly away. The youngest brother became angry and started running after the woodpecker. His brother laughed at him,

'You fool, we still have plenty of wheat here, don't bother running after that cheeky bird!'

But the youngest boy kept running. When he realized that he had lost his way he found himself in a dense forest. He was still looking for the woodpecker but could

not see him anywhere. In his fright he became even more lost. Finally he climbed to the top of a tall tree where he looked around in every direction. He looked north and could see nothing, he looked west and could see nothing there either, he looked east and there he saw something shining brightly. He climbed down from the tree and started to go towards the bright spot.

After a short time he found an opening. In the middle of the opening he found a big fire—a fire as big as a house. Closer he went and oh! My goodness, what do you think was there? The young man gasped as his eyes rested upon a huge giant lying by the fire fast asleep. 'What should I do now?' he asked himself.

If he lied down far from the fire he would catch a cold and if he lied too close to the fire then the giant would discover him and probably kill him, he thought. Quickly he hid in the sleeve of the giant's coat. But, the giant was asleep and did not move until the next morning.

As the giant woke up and struggled to his feet, and adjusted his coat, a child fell down from the sleeve! Well, the young man seemed to be the size of a child to the huge giant. Amazingly enough, the giant did not harm the lad, but he gently picked him up and put him in his lap and took him to his palace. At the palace, he put the young man in a nice bed for a rest. When he awoke the giant told him, 'Now, my son, please consider me as your father from now on. Stay with me and I will give you everything you wish.'

And the young man stayed with the giant who gave him golden and silver clothes as though he were a prince. If he wished for something the giant would draw it in the sand and it would magically appear. As time passed the young man started to feel sad and when the giant noticed this he asked him, 'What is bothering you, my sweet son? You have everything that you could ever want.'

'That is true, my father,' the young man said, 'but I am old enough now and what I really want is to get married.'

'That is fine with me, my dear son, if that is what you wish. There is a round lake not far from here and Elizabeth, the Fairy goes there often to take a bath. She disguises herself as a white dove and flies to the lake at high noon. There she turns into the most beautiful girl that you have ever seen in your life. Go to the lake early in the morning, hide behind a bush and wait until she arrives to take a bath. While she is in the water pick up her dress and carry it back to me. She will beg you to turn back and stay with her but you must not turn back. Do not stop even for a second. Don't worry, she will come after you.'

The next day the young man left home in the early morning, hid behind a bush, beside the lake and waited for the white dove. As the sun rose to its highest point, the dove appeared in the sky and settled on the shore of the lake and before the young man's eyes, it turned into a lovely and very beautiful golden-haired girl. As she dove into the lake to take a bath the lad jumped out from behind the bush, grabbed her golden dress and ran away fast toward the forest. Elizabeth, the Fairy shouted after him, 'Stop, young man, turn back and look at me! But she shouted in vain because the young man did not turn back.

One week passed and then two and the young man became very anxious. It was true that he had Elizabeth, the Fairy's dress but what was the point if he could not have the Fairy herself? He said to the giant, 'Oh, my father, I brought her dress back to you for nothing.'

'Don't worry, Elizabeth, the Fairy will come for her dress. Now go to the pantry and find a walnut. Open its shell and remove the nut. Place Elizabeth, the Fairy's dress inside the nutshell. The young man went to the pantry to fetch a walnut. He split its shell open and put Elizabeth, the Fairy's dress inside. You wouldn't believe it unless you saw how perfectly it fit!

'Now, my son,' said the giant, 'I will sew this walnut in your coat pocket but you must guard it carefully and do not let anyone to take it—not your mother, your father or either of your brothers. If they do, your life will become miserable.'

As the giant sewed the last stitch in the young man's coat pocket a coach arrived at the courtyard drawn by six horses. There was Elizabeth, the Fairy! The giant said, 'Look out the window my son, the beautiful Elizabeth, the Fairy is here, the woman for whom your heart has been longing for so long!'

Elizabeth, the Fairy emerged from the coach and entered the palace. Meanwhile the giant came out to the courtyard and drew many people in the sand and in a flash the courtyard and the palace were full of their guests' chatter and merriment. They went on like this for a long time as Elizabeth, the Fairy and the young man celebrated their wedding.

Some time passed. The young couple lived as happily as a pair of turtledoves until one day the young man seemed sad again. 'What is wrong with you, my sweet son?' The giant asked him, 'You have everything imaginable, what else do you wish?'

'What you say is true, I have everything I could possibly want my father, but my heart is aching for my mother and father and brothers. It has been so long since I have seen them.'

'Fine then, go home, but I warn you that your father thinks that you are dead and when you arrive at your parents home it will be the 30th time that a wake has been held for you. When they realize that you are alive there will be a big celebration with much joy and merriment. And remember to take care of the walnut!'

The giant left the courtyard and with a stick he drew a coach, six horses and servants in the sand. Immediately they appeared live in front of the palace. The young couple sat in the coach, but before they departed the giant told the lad that if at any time he wished to return to the giant, he would only need to draw his wish in the sand and it would be fulfilled.

And so, the lad and Elizabeth, the Fairy departed for the young man's house. Everything that happened to them was just as the giant had said it would. A long table ran through the middle of the courtyard where the young man's parents were sitting and eating with their friends. But nobody was talking! They were still mourning their youngest son! Suddenly a coach turned into their yard and a very elegant man and a strikingly beautiful woman stepped out.

All the people were so surprised. They started guessing as to who this nobleman wearing magnificent golden attire and his companion who was splendidly dressed in silk with a golden dress covered with diamonds could be. The young man walked directly up to his father at the head of the table and greeted him,

'Good day sir, tell me, what is the occasion that calls for such a grand feast?'

'This is a wake for our youngest son, my lord,' said the old man, 'This is the 30th time we have mourned him. Until we die, we will not forget him.'

'How would you recognize your son, if he were here?'

'I would recognize him for the mole under his left arm.' said the old man's wife. And so the young man turned up his left sleeve and said,

'Here is my mole, my dear mother.'

Imagine how wonderfully surprised everyone was! The sadness of the wake quickly turned into joy and mirth! Everybody started to dance. Elizabeth, the Fairy danced too and she danced so beautifully that everyone watched her with great admiration.

'We have never seen such graceful dancing!' the people said.

Elizabeth, the Fairy with her eyes downcast, only said, 'I wish I could dance in the dress that I wore as a girl.'

'And where is your dress?' they asked.

'Oh, it is in a walnut in my husband's pocket and he will never give it to me, not in his life.'

'Do not worry about that,' said the young man's mother, 'I will retrieve it myself.' Wasting no time, she put some sleeping-powder into her son's wine. Upon drinking it, he fell asleep and his mother cut the walnut from his pocket and presented the dress to Elizabeth, the Fairy.

Elizabeth, the Fairy adorned herself in the magical dress and started to dance. What a beauty! Everyone was enchanted! Elizabeth, the Fairy continued dancing and dancing and swirling and swirling when suddenly—can you guess what happened? With one whirl she became a white dove and fluttered up into the branches of a tall tree.

The old man and woman started shouting loudly as they tried to wake their son.

'Wake up, wake up, look at your wife!' But the young man did not wake up. People lifted him and leaned him against the tree, below the branches where the white dove sat. But he still could not wake up. The white dove shed a tear, which dropped on his face, and she said,

'My dear husband, if you would like to see me again in his life, come and find me in the Black-Sorrow country in the city of Johara. That is where I will be.'

Swiftly, the dove withdrew into the darkening sky and the young man's eyes fluttered open. He shouted, 'Come back, come back my beautiful white dove!'

But she did not come back and disappeared in the distance. The poor lad was devastated. He had never heard of the Black-Sorrow country and the city of Johara. What could he do? But he remembered the giant's words, and drew a horse in the sand and just like magic a magnificent horse stood before him. Then he wished to be in the giant's palace. He got on his horse, said good-bye to his parents, and he found himself back with the giant.

'Now my son, the walnut was taken from your pocket, wasn't it?'

'It was, my dear father, what should I do now? Elizabeth, the Fairy said that I should go to the country of Black-Sorrow and to the city of Johara if I ever want to see her again.'

'Oh, my dear son, I have never heard about that country,' said the giant, 'Just stay here with me and forget about Elizabeth, the Fairy'

'Never. I will not rest until I see my beautiful wife again.'

'Very well,' said the giant, 'I will give you my cudgel. I have a brother and a sister. We could not share this cudgel so I kept it. Go to them and take the cudgel with you. They will recognize it and they will know that I sent you. If they can help you they will, if not you must come back to me.'

The giant drew a young filly in the sand and gave some food and gold to the lad and said, 'Go my son, god speed.'

The young man had travelled through seven countries and seven forests when he

finally reached the palace of the giant's brother. While travelling, his filly had become so old that he lost all his teeth. The young lad greeted the giant's brother politely. He explained everything and showed him the cudgel, too. He learned that this man was the King of the Reptiles.

The king said, 'I can see that it was my brother who sent you here. I would like to help you but my animals have just left an hour ago. Tomorrow morning I will call them together.' When they awoke, the king blew his whistle three times and the reptiles came from every direction. The courtyard became full of them and the king said,

'Did any of you hear of the Black-Sorrow country and the city of Johara?' They all answered that although they had crawled through a lot of countries, they had never heard about them.

What could the young man do now? He decided to go to the giant's sister. He went to find his horse but the poor creature was already dead, so he drew another filly in the sand. The young man mounted this horse and slipped away to meet the giant's sister. He rode through seven countries and seven forests when he finally reached the palace of the giant's sister who was the Queen of the birds. He explained everything to her and showed her the cudgel.

And the Queen of the birds told him, 'I would help you, but I do not know anything about the Black-Sorrow country. I wish you would have come earlier as my birds just flew away. Now have your supper and go to bed.'

The young man lay down and the Queen of the birds put a large millstone on him. Then she fetched a golden whip and standing in the middle of the courtyard she cracked the whip and it made such a big noise that earth and sky began thundering loudly and the poor lad was so scared that he kicked the millstone a whole inch into the air.

The Queen of the birds called him from the courtyard, 'Have no fear, my son, I will crack the whip two more times.' And she cracked a second time and this time the poor lad was so afraid that he kicked the millstone a whole foot in the air. And the Queen of the Birds called to him from outside again, 'Have no fear, my son, I will only crack it one last time.'

And she cracked it yet a third time and it made such a huge sound that the poor lad kicked the millstone all the way to the attic. Then the Queen of the birds came into the house and said, 'Well, my son, you can get up now, I will not crack it anymore.'

And at that moment birds started to fly to them from everywhere. From every direction: birds and more birds! They were cawing and chirping so loudly that it was as if a roaring wind had pushed them forth. The poor lad imagined that this was a sign of the end of life on earth!

The Queen asked her birds, 'Who among you has been to the country of Black-Sorrow?'

'Not me, not me, not me.' They said. None of them had ever heard of the Black-Sorrow country.

'I have no choice, I have to return to my giant-father now' said the lad very sorrowfully indeed. As he tried to mount his horse, it grew old and died. Then the poor lad looked at his hands and he realized that he himself was not a young man anymore. He too grew old while he was searching for Elizabeth, the Fairy.

Once again he drew a filly in the sand and mounted him. He wanted to say goodbye to the Queen of the Birds, but at that moment a very tired woodpecker flew into the courtyard. The Queen was angry at the woodpecker and demanded,

'Where have you been? Why are you so late?'

The woodpecker said, 'One of my legs is broken and that is why I am later.'

'Where did this happen to you?'

'In the country of Black-Sorrow, in the city of Johara.' The lad gasped and the Queen said solemnly,

'We need your help Woodpecker.' The woodpecker resisted at first because he was afraid that in the city of Johara someone would break his other leg, too. But the Queen commanded, 'Obey me, and take the lad immediately.' The woodpecker did not have a choice so he let the lad slide onto his back. They flew together through the dark forests and open fields and stormy seas and then to a mountain's top that was so high that it reached the top of the sky.

'Now get off my back as I cannot fly over the mountain with you on me.'

'And how about you? Said the lad, 'How did you fly through here earlier?'

'I flew through a hole,' said the woodpecker.

'Fine, take me through the same hole then.' But the woodpecker did not want to and the poor lad lost his temper and began shouting at him, 'I command that you take me at this moment! I am sure that you were the one who had stolen the golden ear of wheat from my field!'

Oh! The woodpecker was scared when he heard that and he flew with the lad through the mountain hole immediately. As they flew through it, where do you think they arrived? They arrived in the country of Black-Sorrow and they found themselves in the city of Johara. There was a sparkling diamond palace in the city of Johara and it belonged to Elizabeth, the Fairy.

The poor old lad went to the palace where he saw Elizabeth, the Fairy sitting on a golden sofa. She was as beautiful and as young as ever. The old lad greeted her and asked her, 'Do you know who I am beautiful Elizabeth?'

'I will know when you tell me.' She said with a smile.

'I am your husband, beautiful Elizabeth.'

But she started to laugh so heartily that the whole palace echoed with laughter.

'I do not believe you, you are a wrinkled old man and my husband is young and handsome. You can go back to where you came from.'

The poor lad turned toward the door feeling dejected. But Elizabeth, the Fairy ran after him and invited him to her table. 'Eat and drink something before you go.' So the lad ate and drank but his heart was very heavy so he could not really enjoy the meal. When all the plates had been emptied and the old lad was preparing for his journey home, Elizabeth, the Fairy said, 'Now that you have eaten and drank good wine, go to the next room and bathe in the golden bathtub.'

So the poor lad went into the next room and took a bath in the golden bathtub. Soon Elizabeth, the Fairy's maids came into the room and dried him off with golden towels. They combed his hair with golden combs and dressed him in purple garments and wonder of wonders!! The poor old lad had turned into a young man again and he was seventy times more handsome as he'd been before! And Elizabeth, the Fairy happily recognized him and hugged and kissed him.

They held a magnificent feast for everyone in the country of Black-Sorrow. Later they drew a coach with six horses in the sand and did not stop until they reached the palace of the giant. They still live happily even to this day, unless of course they have died.

King Matthias' Shepherd

King Matthias of Hungary was very famous for his love of truth. He had a trustworthy servant, a shepherd, whom he would trust with his life as the shepherd never lied to him. One day King Burkus from the neighbouring kingdom visited King Matthias and they had a splendid supper together. During the dinner King Matthias began to talk about how proud he was of his shepherd as he had never lied in his life – there was no treasure in the world this young man would lie for.

'I don't believe that,' said King Burkus.

'Really? You don't believe me? Well then, let's have a bet.'

'How much will you bet?'

'If you can make my shepherd lie, I will give you half of my country,' said King Matthias, 'but if you are not successful then you'll give me half of your lands'.

They shook hands and King Burkus' daughter, who sat with them, witnessed their wager. They did not talk more about the shepherd. They enjoyed themselves and when the supper was over King Burkus went to his suite. But he could not sleep for hours, as he thought about how he could acquire half of the country of King Matthias.

Finally he remembered that King Matthias had a golden-haired lamb and that the shepherd looked after him. He thought he would go to the village where the shepherd lived and promise him a great treasure for the golden-haired lamb. He was sure that the shepherd would not tell King Matthias the truth about the fate of his beloved lamb.

King Burkus put on peasant's clothes and went to see the shepherd. He greeted him politely,

'Good evening, good fellow.'

'Good evening, Your Majesty,' answered the shepherd.

'How do you know that I am a king?' The surprised King Burkus asked.

'I can see it in your gestures.' The shepherd said.

'Well, you recognized me,' King Burkus said, 'but do you know why I am here?'

'Only if you tell me.'

'I came here to buy the golden-haired lamb from you and I was going to give you so much gold that you could live like a nobleman for the rest of your life.

'I cannot sell him to you, Your Majesty.' The shepherd said. 'What would I tell my king if he asked where the lamb was?'

'Oh, you fool. You could tell him that the wolves took him.'

'I cannot say that, Your Majesty,' the shepherd said, 'I cannot lie to my King.'

'Give me the lamb, shepherd and I will make you a gentleman.'

'I do not want to be a gentleman, Your Majesty. I am a poor fellow but I feel comfortable. If you like the lamb so much you should buy him from my king.'

King Burkus realized that he was talking in vain. He felt frustrated and so he went back to his suite at the palace. He thought and thought about how he could get the golden-haired lamb. Finally he had a good idea. He would send his daughter to the shepherd in the hope that the shepherd would not deny the lamb from her. The princess was as beautiful and splendid as the brightest star in the sky. So King Burkus asked his daughter to do this task for him.

'Fine, dear father, I will try my best.'

And the princess went to the village taking a chest of gold along. The shepherd was herding the flock when the princess approached.

'Good evening, poor shepherd.'

'Good evening, princess. What are you doing here so late in the evening?'

'If you knew, poor shepherd my reason, you would take pity on me! I've had no peace ever since I heard about the golden-haired lamb. My chest is full of gold. Give me the lamb in exchange for it.'

'I cannot do that, Majestic Princess.'

But the princess had also brought the best wines and she offered them to the lad.

'Try these wines, poor shepherd.'

The shepherd drank and became very cheerful. The princess tried her luck again. She opened the top of the chest and showed the bright gold pieces to the poor shepherd.

'Look, these are all yours and you'll receive even more if you give me the golden-haired lamb.'

'I told you already. I cannot do that, Majestic Princess.' The shepherd said. 'I would not give the lamb away for all of the treasures of the world. But if you kiss me once then I would give him to you.'

The princess hesitated for a moment and then quickly kissed the shepherd.

'Now,' she said, 'Kill the lamb as I only need his golden-haired skin.'

The shepherd killed the lamb, pulled off his skin and the princess took it from his hands and ran away with it. She ran home. She was euphoric from joy. And you can imagine how happy the King Burkus was! He could hardly wait until the morning when he would take the golden-haired skin to King Matthias.

'Here is the skin of the golden-haired lamb! Now we will find out whether your shepherd will tell us the truth.'

Meanwhile the shepherd woke up the following morning and as he remembered what he did, he became very ashamed and sad. He knew that the king would hang him for this. What should he do?

He thought that he would go to the king and tell him the truth right away. So he departed. As he was walking on the plain he found a hole in the ground. A squirrel once lived there but now it was empty. He inserted his stick into it and put his hat on the top of the stick. He then stepped back from it as if the stick were King Matthias and he humbly greeted him.

'Good morning, Your Majesty.'

And he answered himself, 'Good morning shepherd. What is the news in the village?'

'There is big trouble, Your Majesty. The golden-haired lamb got lost.'

'This is not true, because other lambs would have been lost then.'

The shepherd sadly pulled his stick from the hole and thought to himself. 'Better to tell the king the truth, he won't believe any lies anyway. He went further and found another hole in the ground. He pushed his stick into it and threw his hat on the top and pretended that the stick was King Matthias.

'Good morning Your Majesty.'

'Good morning, shepherd. What is the news in the village?'

'There is big trouble, Your Majesty. The golden-haired lamb fell into a well and died.'

'This couldn't be true, because every lamb would have fallen in.'

'This is not good,' The shepherd thought to himself. He sadly pulled the stick out of the hole and walked on. And soon he found a third hole on the ground. He shoved his stick into the hole and practiced lying again.

'Good morning, Your Majesty.'

'Good morning, shepherd. What is the news in the village?'

'There is big trouble, Your Majesty. The wolves ate the golden-haired lamb.'

'You lie, because they would have eaten the other lambs too.'

Oh goodness! What should he do? The third lie wasn't going to work either. He decided then and there that he would tell the truth. As soon as he decided this, a strange thing came to his mind and he started to laugh. He became cheerful, put his hat back on his head and was smiling when he appeared in front of King Matthias.

King Matthias was sitting at the table with King Burkus and between them sat the princess. King Burkus was in a very joyous mood. He was looking forward to gaining half of King Matthias' country and he was also looking forward to the shepherd's lie.

'Good morning, Your Majesties and good morning to you too, Princess.'

'Good morning, shepherd. What is the news in the village?' King Matthias asked.

'There is only one thing, Your Majesty. I exchanged the golden-haired lamb for a black-haired lamb.'

'What kind of black-haired lamb?'

'A lamb more beautiful than the golden-haired lamb, Your Majesty. She is as beautiful as the shining sun.'

'Where is that black-haired lamb? Bring her here.'

'I do not have to bring her, Your Majesty, she is sitting here at your table,' and the shepherd gestured towards the princess.

And King Matthias started to laugh and shouted loudly in his joy.

'Very well young man! You told us the truth. I won half of the lands of King Burkus and I will give them to you for your honesty.'

And it happened just like that. The shepherd received half of the lands of King Burkus and when he asked for the hand of the princess, to his greatest joy he received a 'yes' from her. Their marriage was celebrated that very day. Indeed the shepherd was the most fortunate of men and he lived with his bride happily ever after for many years to come.

The Sun's Daughter Princess

Once upon a time, beyond the glass mountains, there lived a king and a queen. This king was so rich that he ruled over two kingdoms; one was nearby and the other was beyond the sea. He had more soldiers in his army than there are blades of grass in the field and stars in the sky. Even though his kingdom spread over two countries and his army of soldiers was large, he was still very unhappy—he did not have any children. He and his queen were very sad. The queen would sigh endlessly in her deep sorrow. Every day she wished for either a baby girl or a boy. The people of the two kingdoms also wished for a child for their queen.

However the wishes of the queen and her people were not in vain! One surprising day the queen gave birth to a baby girl. But what a girl she was! She was so lovely and beautiful that nobody in the whole wide world had seen anybody like her! Her hair was radiant like the bright sun and her eyes were shining like diamonds. People called her the Sun's daughter princess. Oh, you can imagine how happy her parents were and looked after the princess; they gave her bubble baths, smeared her delicate body with different lotions and they even protected her from the wind.

When the beautiful princess grew into a young woman, the king announced in both of his kingdoms that he would welcome any eligible prince into his court so that his daughter could choose her future husband. In no time the neighbouring princes crowded into the king's courtyard as they all wished to have a chance to impress the princess.

'Come, sweet daughter,' the king said. 'Just look at all of the fine princes who have come from the neighbouring kingdoms to win your heart. You are free to choose your husband.'

'Oh father, I don't want to even look at them,' the princess answered, 'please tell them that only the bravest will have a chance with me.'

'As you wish, my daughter, I will tell them,' the king said and he went to the balcony and announced the princess' wish.

He could not even finish what he was saying when all the suitors pulled out their swords and began dueling with one another. Eventually only ten men still stood on their feet. The princess looked out at the dueling men but when her father asked her which prince she liked, she replied,

44

'I do not like any of them my dear father. Fighting with a sword is easy. Any man can do that. I still don't know who is the bravest among them.

'You are right, my daughter,' the king said, 'let's try something else.'

An enormous wild boar had made its home in the king's forest and this boar was so scary that no one dared to cross the forest as they were so afraid of him. The king had offered different rewards to have this animal killed but nobody had ever been successful. He announced that he would give one of his kingdoms and his daughter's hand in marriage to the man who would kill the wild boar.

So the princes set off to the forest to find the wild boar. The princess disguised herself as a man so that nobody would recognize her. As the hunters reached the forest a handsome young man dressed in black clothes joined them and asked one of the king's guards if he knew where the wild boar roamed in the forest. The guard was surprised,

'We are looking for the great boar ourselves. You too would like to try your luck?'

'Yes, that's right, I would.'

The princess overheard this conversation and became very interested in this handsome young man. She secretly hoped that he would kill the wild boar. She wanted him as her husband even though it was obvious by his clothing that he was from the lower classes.

Meanwhile the princes had scattered in every direction and the young man wearing black clothes stood under a big tree. The princess hid behind a tall bush watching him. After a little time had passed, all the princes, one after the other, sneaked up to the young man under the tree and offered him a sack of gold if he would give them the head of the wild boar. The young man's answer was the same every time— he could not promise anything for the moment, but they could discuss it further once he had killed the wild boar.

When the princes had gone back into the forest the princess, who was still disguised as a man, came out from behind the bush and asked the young man in black clothes,

'Why did you not accept the gold they offered you?' She looked straight into his defiant eyes, 'What a fool! You could have bought three kingdoms and be a rich man!'

'But I do not want their gold—all that matters to me is that the king's daughter becomes my bride! I don't even care about one of the king's countries, as long as I can have his daughter!'

Suddenly they stopped talking. From nowhere an enormous and angry wild boar bolted out of the trees and ran towards them grunting menacingly and snapping his tusks back and forth as he looked for a prey. The princess ran to the top of a high rock to see what would happen next. The young man did not stand around either, he climbed up an oak tree as fast as he could just as the wild boar was about to claw him. In the tree he shook the branches so much that the acorns fell to the ground. The wild boar jumped into the acorns and started to eat. He ate so much that he could hardly move. He lay down under the tree and fell asleep snoring so loudly that the sound created a stormy wind and all the branches of the tree were bent.

Then the young man in black clothes climbed down the tree and tiptoed next to the wild boar. He gently scratched its furry back with his knife so that he would continue to sleep well. In a flash he pulled out his sword and with one swift stroke he cut off the wild boar's head. He put it on his sword and walked towards the hunting lodge where the king was waiting for the bravest of all the men.

'Behold, Your Majesty, here is the head of the wild boar!'

'Who are you?' The king asked him, as he had not seen the young man earlier.

'I cannot tell you just yet, Your Majesty, but you will know soon enough.

Meanwhile the princes had arrived at the hunting lodge. They all claimed that the wild boar was not killed by this young man in black but that, in fact, they had killed it!

'Who killed it?' Asked the king, 'I need to know for sure!'

'I did, I did!' shouted the many princes.

But then the princess came forward and told the king,

'Do not believe them, my dear father, I saw it with my own eyes that this young man in black killed the wild boar. I also overheard that all of these princes offered him a sack of gold for the head.'

The king turned to the young man in black. 'So be it. Then this man will have my daughter in marriage and one of my kingdoms.'

'And I will be very happy to have him as my husband.' The princess said.

The young man took an iron ring from his finger and said to the princess,

'Take this ring, dear princess and put it on your finger. I will return to my country now, but I will come for you soon. Take good care of this ring and always keep it with you.'

And the Sun's daughter princess then also took off a golden ring from her finger and said to the young man,

'You, too put this ring on your finger and I will see you soon.'

As the young man and the princess said good-bye, they held each other's hands tightly. Before he made his way down the pathway away from the palace, the king burst out,

'I cannot allow my future son-in-law to return to his country on foot. Fetch my fastest horse!' The disgraced princes overheard this and quickly planned a trap for the young man. They promised many gold pieces to the barn master if he would give him the wildest horse. The barn master happily accepted the offer and... can you imagine what happened? He really got the wildest horse, which had drunk dragon milk when he was young and no man yet had broken him. The king became very angry when he saw this trick but the young man in black calmed him down,

'Do not worry, Your Majesty, even if this horse did drink dragon-milk, I can still ride him!'

'I can tell you, my son that this one really did that!'

The king did not even finish his sentence when the young man tipped his hat and leapt onto the wild horse. He pressed his legs tightly against its sides, struck his head three times with his sword and rode him three times around the forest. When he finally rode back to say good-bye to the princess and the king, the horse's whole body was covered by sweat.

'Well,' said the king, 'this young man could not possibly be a poor peasant-boy— he rode this horse as if he were a king.'

Some time went by when one day a messenger arrived from the Black Kingdom with a note for the princess' father. The message was very frightening indeed. Unless the king would give his daughter's hand in marriage to the Black King he would declare war on the King's two kingdoms.

You can imagine how frightened the old king became! He ran to his daughter, explained everything to her,

'Now my sweet daughter, what should I tell the messenger?'

The princess replied, 'Tell him, my dear father, that I will marry only the young man in black clothes and nobody else.'

No sooner had the king conveyed his daughter's decision to the messenger than the Black King's army began marching into the city. Soon the old king's palace was full of invading soldiers. Their general repeated the Black King's demands. The king, more frightened than ever, ran to his daughter again, 'Think about it carefully my sweet daughter, the Black King has a very big army.' But she was adamant, 'I would not care if he had all the soldiers in the world, I will not marry him.'

They took this message to the Black King who was waiting at the city's border. When he heard the princess' answer he walked straight to the palace. He was wearing such a bright outfit that people had to shield their eyes. He went directly to the princess and asked her, 'Would you marry me princess?'

'No, I will not.' she said.

At that moment the Black King took off his overcoat and, hard though it is to believe he was wearing a black outfit!

'And how about now, would you marry me?' He asked the princess again. She squinted in disbelief,

'So, it's you?' And she saw her ring on his finger.

'Yes, it's me...would you marry me?'

'I will! I will!' shouted the princess happily and excitedly.

Ah, how happy they were! The entire court celebrated their wedding. It lasted for seven weeks and everybody was singing and dancing. I was there too and I danced too. Finally I ran home and brought this tale to you. I hope you liked it.

The Poor Man and the Fox

Once upon a time, a very long time ago, there lived a poor man whose only possessions were two oxen and a small patch of land. This land was far away, at the border of a large forest. Sometimes it yielded some wheat but other times it did not. One day the poor man went to his land to plough it and while he was ploughing he suddenly heard a terrible roaring and a frightened whining from the forest. He ran in the direction of the sounds to see what it was. And what do you think he saw? A huge bear was fighting with a tiny rabbit. When the poor man saw this, he began to laugh so much that the whole forest echoed.

'I've seen a lot of strange things in my life but never have I seen a bear fighting with a rabbit.' But when the bear heard the poor man's words, he said angrily,

'Just wait, cursed fellow, you won't laugh for long. I'll kill your two oxen and you too!'

Of course the poor soul's mood changed immediately and he begged the bear not to kill him at least until the evening. He needed to break up his land and sow it with wheat in order to leave something for his children to eat.

'Agreed,' the bear said. 'I'll leave you alone until the evening. I'll let you go break up your soil for now.'

The poor man went back to his plough but he was so sad that he could hardly work. But then a fox appeared from the trees in the nearby forest.

'Why are you so sad, poor fellow?'

'Don't even ask me, fox. My sorrow is so deep! When I finish this ploughing, a bear will come to kill me and my oxen too.'

And the fox said,

'Do not be sad, poor fellow. I could help you but how would you pay me?'

'I don't have anything.' The poor man said.

'Well, actually, you still have something,' the fox said, ' if you have oxen I am sure that you have a rooster and hens too.'

'Well really,' the poor soul thought, 'those nine hens and rooster belong to my wife and I am about to promise them to a fox! I must be the worst man who walks this earth!'

But they shook hands and the poor man promised the rooster and the nine hens to the fox. And the fox told him,

'Listen to me, poor fellow. I will hide myself behind a bush here, and when the bear comes I will imitate the sound of a horn. The bear will think hunters are coming and he'll ask you to hide him somewhere. You can hide the bear in a sack that I will bring you. Once he's in the sack, I will come out from behind the bush and I'll ask you, 'what's in the sack, poor fellow?' And you say, a 'stump'. 'I don't believe you' I will say. And then take your axe and hit the bear's head with all of your strength.'

When the fox had finished he leapt away back into the forest. One hour hadn't not pass when he came back with a sack for the poor man. He then hid himself behind a bush and waited for the bear. When the poor man finished ploughing, the bear approached him, growling,

'Now your life is finished.'

But the bear suddenly became very afraid when he heard the sound of a horn coming from behind the bush.

'Oh my! Please, poor man, I won't hurt you, if only you'll help me by hiding me somewhere.'

'I don't know where could I hide you,' the poor man said, 'maybe you can hide yourself in this sack.'

'Perfect,' the bear said as he scurried inside.

The poor man quickly tied up the opening. As was previously agreed upon, the fox now came along and asked the poor man what he had in the sack. The fox did not believe that there was only a stump inside and so the poor man took his axe and swung with all his might. A soft moan could be heard as the sack fell over.

'Now that I've saved your life,' the fox said. 'don't forget what you promised me. Tomorrow I will meet you to gather the nine hens and the rooster that you owe me.'

'Yes, do come tomorrow, master fox, come to my house.' But the poor man was thinking, 'I will be more sly than you, I've learned something from you today.'

The poor man went home, had his supper and went to bed. By dawn, when the rooster began to crow, the fox was already there, knocking on the front door.

'Hello, poor fellow, I've come for the nine hens and the rooster.'

'Wait a second, master fox,' said the poor man, 'I need to dress properly. It's chilly today.'

But he didn't get dressed at all, but stayed in his bed and began to bark like a fox-hound. The fox shouted, 'Do you have hounds, poor man?'

'Funny, I don't know where they're from but two hounds came into my room yesterday evening and now I can hardly hold them back. They have smelled you and now they want to catch you.'

The fox became very afraid and he shouted,

'Please, my friend hold them back until I run away!' He did not want any rooster or hen anymore and he ran off as fast as his legs could carry him. Maybe he is still running. And this is the end of my tale.

The Golden-Haired Children

Once upon a time, a very long time ago, far beyond the end of the world, there lived a young king, who had a beautiful wife. They were married for only one year when the king had to go to war. While he fought in a foreign land, his wife gave birth to two golden-haired children; one was a girl and the other a boy. Oh, you cannot imagine what happened next! The young queen mother had not even looked at her beautiful newborn children when a wicked old woman, who was the king's nursemaid, stole the golden-haired babies and placed two puppies in their place! This wicked old woman locked the children in a wooden box and threw the box into the sea. And why do you think she did this? She wanted the king to marry her daughter. And really, as you will soon see, everything happened as she wished.

When the king came back from the war and heard that his wife had given birth to two puppies he became so furious that he had her sewn into a buffalo-skin and had a hole dug in front of the local church where she was placed. He also ordered his servants to spit on the queen when they went to church as he felt humiliated by having two puppies as heirs. And of course he ended up marrying the wicked woman's daughter.

Do not worry, the truth will soon be known. First let us see what happened to the golden-haired children. The box floated on the waves, sometimes half submerged, other times resting on the surface. Eventually it was caught by an old fisherman. The fisherman took the box home, opened it with his wife and by Jove! They were overjoyed when they saw the two golden-haired babies! You see, they did not have any children and they were very happy to receive such a wonderful present. They looked after the children and raised them as their own. The golden-haired children of course did not know that they were born as a prince and a princess.

Time passed by and one day the fisherman's wife sent the little princess to the well to fetch some water. She had not walked very far when the jug she was carrying fell to the ground and broke into a thousand pieces. She cried but when she got home the fisherman's wife was not angry with her, instead she gave her another jug. So the little girl went on her way again and although she was very careful, the jug slipped from her tiny hands again and shattered on the ground below.

She ran home crying but the fisherman's wife did not scold her.

'If you were my daughter, now I would have beaten you for this'.

The little girl was amazed, she couldn't even say a word she was so surprised to hear that she was not the fisherman's wife's daughter! Until that time she thought that the fisherman's wife was her mother. In the evening when her brother came home from school she told him what happened. Her brother was also surprised and he said to her,

'If this is true that the fisherman is not our father and the fisherman's wife is not our mother then we must go and find our real parents.'

So they decided to leave their foster parents. As you can imagine, the old couple became very sad when they heard what the children had decided to do. They cried and begged them not to leave but the children thanked them for their love and care and said good-bye to them. The fisherman's wife baked them three scones and the fisherman gave them three pieces of silver coin. And so they departed.

They had hardly left the border of their village when an old beggar asked them to stop,

'Good children, I beg you, give me something to eat.'

The golden-haired prince took out one of the scones and a silver coin from his bag and gave these to the beggar. They continued their journey. But they did not go far when another old beggar came to them and asked for some food. And the prince again gave him a piece of silver coin and a piece of scone. And they went further when the third old beggar stopped them.

'For love of God, my children, please give me something to eat.'

They only had one piece of silver coin left and one piece of scone. Still the young prince gave both to the old beggar. After the beggar had thanked them, the little girl said,

'I am so hungry, my dear brother. Please have a look in your bag to see if we have any breadcrumbs there.'

The prince looked in his bag, and wonder of wonders! The three pieces of scones and the three pieces of silver coins were in his bag! They sat down under a tree to eat when an old man appeared in front of them.

'What are you doing, my golden-haired children?' he asked.

The young prince answered,

'We are looking for our father and mother.'

'I heard about you. You gave your food and money to three old beggars. One good turn deserves another.' And the old man shouted out loud,

'Hey, Jethro, come here at once!'

At that moment a little man, a goblin, appeared in front of them. His beard reached the ground.

'What can I do for you, my master?'

'I want you to take these children back to the city where their father lives. In an exchange you will receive two human souls.'

And Jethro the goblin tumbled head over heels and what do you know? He became a magic steed.

'Get on my back,' he said to the golden-haired children. And when they were safely atop, the magic steed jumped in the air and flew as fast as a thought. In a flash he arrived at the border of the king's city, where he turned back into a goblin again. And he said to the children,

'Go to the church, but once you are there do not do what other people do. Just go inside. The king himself will be in the church. When he sees you he will invite you for supper at his palace. He will be very pleased and will offer you anything you wish. You should ask for nothing more than a piece of land near the city that is just large enough for your servant to cartwheel on for an hour'.

As the children went towards the church they saw that people were spitting on a woman who was dug into the earth up to her waist. The children were sad as they passed by her. They would not spit on her if their lives depended on it! As soon as they stepped in the church the chamber became brightly lit from the glow of the children's golden hair. Everyone noticed, including the king, who asked the children,

'I was told that you did not spit on the woman in the buffalo-skin. Do you know that it was me who ordered everybody to spit on her when they arrived at church?'

And the young prince answered him,

'Forgive us, Your Majesty, we did not know about your order because we have come from a foreign land. But even if we knew we would never have spit on that woman. She has not hurt either of us.'

The boy's bold answer pleased the king.

'Come to my palace and have supper with me.'

And the golden-haired children accompanied the king to his palace. The king could not take his eyes off them. He kept sighing ,

'Oh, my God, if only I had these beautiful children!'

And they all sat down for supper but the queen and her mother, the old wicked woman, did not join them. They became sick, and were both shivering when they saw the two golden-haired children. The king did not mind their absences and he was very happy in the children's company. He gave them the tastiest bites and when the supper was over he told them,

'My dear children, I am in a very good mood now, you can ask for anything and I will fulfill your wishes.'

And the children asked for nothing else except what Jethro the goblin had suggested.

When the king heard their request he said,

'I do not mind if your servant cartwheels for even three hours—I have a lot of land.' After supper the children went back to see Jethro. They went to bed and when they woke up the next morning the king was already waiting for them with his wife and with his mother-in-law.

'Now, my son, where is your servant?' the king asked the golden-haired boy.

And the prince whistled once,

'Hey, Jethro, come here!'

At once Jethro the goblin appeared before them. And the king said,

'Listen, Jethro, the land that you will cartwheel on for three hours will be given to your young master.'

And Jethro said,

'Even one hour is good enough for me, Your Majesty.' And he turned into a gypsy boy and started cart wheeling down the road! Both the children laughed with glee as they watched their funny servant tumbling feet overhead into the surrounding hills. In one hour he had covered three hundred and ninety nine miles!

When the old wicked woman realized this she became scared and whispered to her daughter,

'Listen, this little man may be dangerous for us. I suggest you praise the land the children just received from the king. But tell them it would be even more beautiful if they brought the golden castle to their new land from the Boiling Seas.

The queen repeated this suggestion to the children, word for word. When the king departed and went back to his palace, Jethro the goblin asked the children,

'What did the queen tell you?'

After the goblin heard the story he said,

'Oh, how wicked she and her mother are! I know what they want—they want to destroy you. Still, we will go to the golden castle and bring it back here tonight!'

When the evening came Jethro the goblin tumbled head over heels and turned into a magic steed again. As soon as the young prince had leapt onto his back, the steed jumped in the air and flew away like a bird. In a twinkle they arrived at the Boiling Seas and landed in front of the golden castle. The valiant steed kicked the door and in a blink the castle had turned into a golden apple!

'Put this golden apple in your pocket, my little master!'

The young prince put it in his pocket and by dawn they had arrived safely home again. When they were home the golden castle sparkled brilliantly in its new place on the children's land. The golden-haired children and the goblin held hands and danced as the sun rose into the sky.

When the old wicked woman saw the golden castle she was so upset that she shivered in her skin. She told her daughter,

'Listen, this little man will cause us a lot of trouble if we are not careful. I'm telling you to go and praise the golden castle and the two children. Tell them that the castle is really beautiful but it could be even more beautiful if they were to bring the twenty-four golden apple trees from the Red Sea.'

And the queen repeated this suggestion three times to the golden-haired prince. And the young prince told this story to Jethro.

'Very well, my master, we will bring the twenty-four golden trees too, although they are guarded by twenty four dragons.'

Then he tumbled head over heels again and turned into a magic steed. The young prince jumped onto his back and in a twinkle they arrived at the Red Sea. All twenty-four dragons spewed flames at them but Jethro the goblin blew sleepy-wind back towards them and the twenty-four dragons fell asleep. So the prince and Jethro took the twenty-four golden apple trees and returned with them safely home.

Oh, my God! You can imagine how upset the old wicked woman was when she saw the twenty-four golden trees in the morning! She ran to her daughter and told her,

'Listen, this Jethro is more clever than I thought. Go to the two children and we shall try something else. Tell them that their land will be even more beautiful if they bring twenty-four singing branches from the twenty-four singing trees. These trees are by the Black Sea. Try to convince them to hang those singing branches on the golden apple trees to make their garden even more beautiful.'

When the little prince had heard this from the wicked woman, he wanted to leave immediately but Jethro the goblin said,

'This is our most difficult task, my little master as the singing trees lie beyond the ugly ogre, Colossus, and the problem is that up to now nobody was ever able to pass by him alive. But we will try.'

And Jethro the goblin became the magical steed and he and the young prince flew over many countries and forests. Suddenly the steed came down to earth and said,

'You can get off me now, my little master. Not far from here you will find Colossus who is taller than the highest mountain and who has two faces and two mouths

and he has such big teeth and they look like steel flag poles. And if you want to pass by him you have to go through those teeth! Now listen to me carefully. I will turn into a single grain of poppy-seed. Put the poppy seed in your pocket. If Colossus knew that I was with you he would crunch both of us and we would be even tinier than a grain of poppy-seed. Unfortunately you have to walk through his two mouths. So trick him— praise him to high heaven as you have never praised anyone in your life.'

As Jethro the goblin finished saying these words he turned into a single grain of poppy-seed, which the prince put in his pocket before making his way towards the ogre. He was walking along confidently when all of a sudden he caught sight of the famous, ugly ogre, Colossus! The young prince had even seen a twenty-four-headed dragon but he had never seen such a horrible, ugly ogre like Colossus. He was certainly the most ugly creature that he had ever laid eyes on! A lump grew in his throat, but he stood boldly in front of the ogre and greeted him,

'Good evening, my dear old man!'

'The same to you, my son.'

'My dear man' the prince said, 'I have never seen a more handsome old gentleman than you! I wish I could see your other face, as well.'

And Colossus said,

'I cannot turn my head, my son but if you climb up to my face I will let you go through my mouth to the other side. I have to confess to you that I have never seen such a handsome young man in my life as you.'

Colossus was so pleased with the prince that he lay on his back to make it easier for him to walk up to his mouth. And the prince did just that—he quickly ran up the ogre's body until he reached his mouth. Colossus opened it and the prince climbed in and went through his gigantic teeth until he reached his mouth on the other side! He jumped out and ran down from the ogre's body to the other side. Finally he jumped down to the ground and ran away from the ogre as far as he could. Then the single grain of poppy-seed leapt out of his pocket and turned into a magic steed again.

The prince got on the steed's back and they flew all the way to the shores of the Black Sea. Jethro's brother lived there. They had not seen each other for three hundred and ninety years as neither of them could get part Colossus.

'How did you get here?' his brother asked in a shock.

'No time to answer now,' said Jethro 'but please help us and fetch twenty-four branches of the singing trees.'

'Yes, my dear brother, I'll do anything. Take a rest, both of you. You can sleep an hour and while you are sleeping I will bring you the singing branches.'

And he got into his boat and pushed it so hard that it landed at the other side of the Black Sea within an instant. He found the magical garden and the twenty-four singing trees. A twenty-four-headed dragon guarded each of the trees! Luckily for Jethro's brother, the dragons were asleep and they only woke up when he tore the singing branches from the trees. As he tore each branch off trees, the sky and the earth thundered loudly. The dragons woke up and flew after Jethro's brother. He managed to escape by jumping in his boat and pushing it so hard that it landed at the other side of the sea right in front of his house.

He woke up his brother and the prince and gave them the twenty-four singing branches. The prince couldn't believe his eyes and took them happily. He thanked Jethro's brother for his courage and then they said good-bye to him. They made their way back home but they had to cross Colossus again!

As they approached the ogre, Jethro turned himself into a single grain of poppy-seed again and the prince put it in his pocket. When he got close to Colossus the young prince shouted to him,

'I was travelling to many far-away places but I have never met such a nice gentleman as you!'

'Fine fine,' said Colossus 'but are you sure you are not mocking me?'

'I would never do that,' the prince said emphatically.

'Very well then. Go through my two mouths quickly.'

The prince went through again Colossus's two mouths, jumped on the ground from his front mouth and when he was far enough from the ogre the single grain of poppy-seed leapt out of his pocket and turned into a magic steed. The prince jumped on his back and the steed told him,

'Now, my little master turn your head back towards Colossus and shout to him that you had never seen such an ugly ogre as he!'

And the prince without waiting for even a second turned his head towards Colossus and shouted at him,

'Hey, Colossus, I have never seen such an ugly ogre as you!'

Oh, you cannot imagine how angry Colossus became with them! He was trembling he was so angry and fumed with rage.

He screamed at them 'Hey Jethro, you goblin, I should have known that it was you behind this trick but if I knew that you were in my mouth I would have crunched you between my teeth and swallowed!' And as he trembled and fumed with rage all of the sudden he turned into a strong wind and became a tornado. And since then Colossus could never turn back into an ogre. He will forever remain the most violent of all the winds.

The golden-haired prince and Jethro the goblin arrived safely home by morning and when the old wicked woman woke up the twenty-four branches were already singing on the golden apple trees and the whole city came to the children's palace to admire this miracle, except the wicked woman and her daughter. They were shivering and fuming in their anger.

And Jethro the goblin told the prince,

'Now, my little master you can invite the king and his court for supper.'

And he just kicked the side of the fireplace in the kitchen and twenty-four cooks jumped out of it. And they cooked and baked the whole day and prepared an excellent meal. By the evening the king and his court came to the golden castle and Jethro the goblin had everybody sit in his proper place. The king sat at the head table and the queen and her mother tried to take their places at his side. But when they tried to sit their chairs jumped up in the air and they both fell on the ground. The king laughed out loud seeing them.

And Jethro the goblin said,

'Your Majesty, I will bring here another woman in a second to sit beside you, and you will see the chair will stay in its place.'

He ran to the church and cut open the real queen from the buffalo-skin, put her on his lap and carried her to the golden castle. In the palace he placed her beside the king and said,

'This woman suits you perfectly, Your Majesty! I hereby now announce it to everyone that this woman did not give birth to two puppies but she gave birth to these two golden-haired children!'

And he told the children's story to the king and his court. And the king immediately knelt down in front of his real wife and asked for her forgiveness. The old wicked woman and her daughter were still shivering in their fear. Jethro the goblin tumbled head over heels and turned into a billy-goat. He put the old woman on one of his horns, put her daughter on his other horn and said,

'My old master promised me these two souls - the old wicked woman and her daughter—were going to be mine so I take them now!'

And he disappeared with them as if the earth had swallowed them up. He did not stop until he reached the entrance of hell and there he threw the two women down into it. When he came back there was a big feast in the golden castle. The twenty-four branches were singing, the court musicians were playing music and everybody was dancing, including of course the king and his queen. I was there and danced, too. After a while I ran home and brought this tale to you.

The Clever Girl

Once upon a time in the land beyond the Seven Seas there lived a clever girl. She was so bright that even the king had heard about her. Since the king wanted to marry, he decided he was going to marry a girl who was not only beautiful but smart as well.

One day, he sent his servants to escort the clever girl to his palace. He greeted her and said, 'I heard about how clever you are. I want to find out whether this is really true, so I prepared three tasks for you. First, I have a hundred year old thread in my attic, can you spin a golden thread from it?'

The girl answered, 'Your Majesty, my father has a hundred year old millstone, if you can make a spindle from it, I will spin you the golden thread.'

The king very much liked this answer.

'Very good. You answered well on the first task. Now I will ask you to do something else. I have one hundred jugs in my attic, all with holes. Can you patch them all?'

'I will be happy to do that,' said the girl, 'But, your Majesty, if I were to put a patch outside the jugs, they would look ugly. First you must turn them inside out then I will patch them, as you requested.'

The king smiled again and said, 'Your second answer was very clever, indeed. Now I will give you the final task. If you can solve it, here is my hand, I will marry you.'

'As you please, Your Majesty.'

'Fine. Here is my last request: bring me a present. Bring it and don't bring it. I will have it and not have it.'

The girl thought for a while then went into the kitchen. There she asked the cook for two baskets. She took the baskets to the courtyard where some doves were flying. She then caught one of the doves. She put the dove in one basket and covered it with the other basket then took them to the king.

'Here is your present, Your Majesty,' she said.

The king took the two baskets and tried to take a look inside. He lifted the top basket. At that moment the dove flew away.

'See, Your Majesty, I brought it and I did not, you had it and you did not.'

The king laughed out loud and as he was already in love with the girl, he married her the very same day. They had a feast that lasted for two whole weeks.

I was there and danced a lot too. If you do not believe it, ask the king yourself!

The Golden Stick

Once upon a time, a very long time ago, there lived a king and his three sons. All three sons were planning to leave their father's kingdom and try their luck in the world. Each prince would travel in a different direction. The eldest would go west where there were forests full of tall golden trees and he would collect their golden leaves. The middle son would go north to collect precious stones with colours that no one had ever before seen. And the youngest wanted to go to sea to learn more about the world.

On a clear day, when there was a gentle breeze in the air, the old king stood for a long time watching as his youngest son sailed away on a huge ship until it disappeared on the horizon.

The young prince travelled for over a year without seeing any dry land. He and his crew ate all their food supplies and were beginning to starve when suddenly they were lucky enough to caught sight of a rocky shore.

The prince went ashore and began to look around. He walked and walked without knowing where he was headed, until he became very sleepy and stopped to take a rest. He fell asleep on a large rock.

He slept for more than a day and as he woke up someone was tenderly caressing his face! He opened his eyes and ...wonder of wonders! A girl who was as beautiful as the brightest stars in the night sky was kneeling over him. She was a fairy, you see. She asked the prince,

'How did you get here?' The prince told her everything about his travels. 'Come, let's go and see my mother, she will have food for you and your crew.' Her mother, who was the Queen of the fairies, took a table-cloth from her chest drawer and said to it, 'Fairy-cloth, I command you to bring forth food and drinks, right away!'

And in a flash, delicious food and drinks appeared on the fairy-cloth. Plenty of food for everyone! The prince ate and saved some food for his crew as well. He thanked the queen very much for her generosity and said good-bye to her. Finally he turned to the princess and said,

'If I come back for you, my fairy princess, will you come with me?'

'Yes, come back, please come back and I will go with you', said the princess. And she gave the fairy-cloth to the prince as a present. The prince returned to his ship and they sailed away until all they could see was sky and water. After many days they

reached an island and the prince went ashore and laid the fairy-cloth on the ground. He said,

'Fairy-cloth, I command you to bring forth food and drinks, right away!' And in the blink of an eye delicious food and drinks appeared on the fairy-cloth. The prince started to eat and while he was eating, an old woman appeared in front of him and begged him to give her a little food in the name of God. The prince said,

'Please, have a seat and make yourself comfortable. Have as much food and drink as you wish. There is plenty for both of us.' The old woman sat down and began to eat but then slowly something invisible seemed to lift her up into the air. And in a flash she had turned into a beautiful fairy!

'You were lucky that you gave me something to eat, prince. If you hadn't given me food I would have taken away your fairy-cloth. Because you were so good to me, I have a gift for you.' And she presented a cloak of many colours to the amazed prince.

'If you shake this cloak and a green patch falls on the ground, there will be a beautiful garden. Where a blue patch falls, there will be a big lake and where a white patch falls will appear a beautiful diamond palace! But if you clap your hands and say, 'garden, lake and palace disappear', then they will become a cloak once again.'

The prince politely thanked her for this mysterious present even though he wasn't sure what he would need it for! He went back to his ship and set sail. It wasn't long until they reached yet another island. The prince went ashore, put his fairy-cloth on the ground, asked for food and drinks again and started to eat. While he was eating an old man came to him and begged him to give him a piece of bread in the name of God. The prince gave him plenty of food and a drink and they had a friendly dinner together.

'Now my dear prince,' said the old man, 'your kindness deserves kindness in return. Here is a golden stick. Take it. As you can see it has a silver knob at its end. You can screw the knob off, and then on your command, as many soldiers will march out from the stick as you wish. They can even occupy a whole country. And if you don't need them anymore, just give them a command to return into the golden stick and they will march smartly right back where they came from!'

After thanking the old man for the golden stick, the prince decided to set sail towards his homeland. He stopped only to ask the fairy princess to accompany him on his ship. She happily packed her things and then they sailed home together. When the prince's ship reached the shores of his father's palace the old king was running toward the ship screaming,

'Turn back, my son, turn back! Our enemy has taken away my kingdom!' The prince screwed off the silver knob of his golden stick and, to everyone's astonishment, an army of soldiers came marching out. The earth almost trembling beneath their boots. And the soldiers attacked the enemy and forced them to retreat. You can imagine how happy the old king was now!

'Well,' the king said, 'you brought the most valuable treasure, my sweet son. Your eldest brother brought a lot of golden leaves but the enemy took them all. Your middle brother brought precious stones, his ship was full with them but the enemy took them away, as well. You brought only a golden stick but it saved our kingdom!'

Then the king's face grew worried once again, 'Our country is safe now, but these soldiers will eat all of our food supplies.'

'Don't worry about that, my dear father,' the prince said, 'we don't have to feed them.' With that he shouted to the soldiers, 'Back!' and they all marched smartly into the golden stick.

Then the prince took the lovely fairy princess to a beautiful place in the country and shook his colourful cloak. A green patch fluttered to the ground. Instantly it turned into a beautiful garden, blossom of every colour erupting from the soil. As a blue patch hit the ground it turned into a glistening lake full of gliding swans, and a white patch from the cloak transformed into a glittering diamond palace. Oh, what a sight it was! People from everywhere came to admire it.

And the prince married his fairy princess and the wedding celebration lasted seven days and seven nights. And they still live happily even to this day.

Jack Beetle

A very long time ago there lived a miller and a cobbler. They were poorer than a church mouse. Sometimes they had a little something to eat but often they didn't. One day the miller said to the cobbler,

'I really don't want to be hungry anymore, my friend. We must figure out how to make some money.'

'You are right,' said the cobbler, 'Let's think.'

And so for hours they tossed different ideas back and forth, finally deciding that the miller would secretly take the rich lord's six beautiful horses to the forest and tie them to a tree with some rope. Of course the rich lord would become very upset when he discovered that his horses had gone missing. Now the cobbler had an old, thick book that was full of useless information. They decided that he would offer his services saying that he would be able to find the rich lord's horses by consulting his magical book. The cobbler's services would then be handsomely rewarded, he hoped.

And so they executed the plan. Dawn was misty and strangely lit as the miller led off six gently neighing horses into the darkest forest and tied them to an enormous oak tree. The following morning, when the rich lord's servants found the stables empty, a troop of men were sent to search throughout the land, in the near-by towns, and over the hills. But the horses could not be found.

When the cobbler heard how desperate the rich lord had become he visited his mansion saying,

'So sorry to hear about your horses, my lord. However I am a man with magical powers at my disposal and I think I can be of your service. However I require a reasonable payment.'

The rich lord's desperation turned into a glimmer of hope and he promised the cobbler three hundred golden pieces if he could discover the whereabouts of his horses. The cobbler took out his magical book and began to read intently, his finger tracing the words, and murmuring to himself.

When he had finished he said,

'There is a spring in the neighbouring forest and beside the spring there is an enormous oak tree. Your horses are tied up there.'

The rich lord ordered his men off to this spot. When they found the big oak tree beside the spring, they were astonished to find the six beautiful horses. The rich lord

was overjoyed! He immediately paid three hundred golden pieces to the cobbler. And the news spread throughout the whole country that Jack Beetle – for that is our cobbler's name – had a magical book that had all of the answers to all of the questions in the world.

The king became very happy upon hearing about this magical man because the queen had lost her favourite ring that very day. She was a delicate soul and by the loss she was devastated. She cried and cried and the doctors reported to the king that the queen's ring had to be found or they could not guarantee her majesty would live to see the third sunrise! So it was very serious indeed. The king immediately sent for the reputed master Beetle.

The golden coach driven by six beautiful horses arrived at the cobbler's house and the marshal stepped off. He reported to master Beetle that the king wished to see him that morning. 'There's big trouble at the court, sir. Big trouble,' he said, and 'you're the only one who can help.'

Poor master Beetle! How scared he was! His face turned green and blue and his whole body trembled like an aspen leaf. He would be found out! He looked for excuses and feigned humility saying that he wasn't very wise and that he had lost his magical book earlier that day.

'Whether you are wise or not, master Beetle,' the marshal said, 'you must come with me or the king will chop off my head!'

So the cobbler had to go. Teary-eyed, he said good-bye to his wife, his children and his best friend, the miller, sure that none would ever see him again.

The golden coach flew along the country lanes. The cobbler sat on its velvet seats wordless and silent.

As soon as they arrived at the court the king greeted him warmly,

'You are so very welcome here, wondrous Jack Beetle!' But then his voice became somber as he moved onto the business at hand. 'A couple of days ago the queen's favourite ring disappeared. And the upheaval ever since is wearing us all down! If you find it, master Beetle, then I will reward you with six cart loads of gold.' Jack did all he could think to do, he bowed and smiled.

'I will do my best, Your Majesty, but I cannot guarantee my success.' The cobbler replied feebly.'

He asked the king to lock him into a room for three days because he needed time and space to think. The king agreed and master Beetle was given one of the most beautiful rooms in the palace and plenty of food. One day passed but the cobbler could not come up with anything. The second day passed and when the third day arrived poor Master Beetle was distraught.

'Oh my God,' he thought, 'my good life will soon be finished. If I cannot find the ring, I'll lose my head!' On the third evening the footman brought him his supper and the poor cobbler thought he would count how many dishes he would eat for the last time. And when the footman came with the first course, master Beetle said out loud,

'Here comes the first one.'

Hearing this, the footman became so frightened that he nearly dropped the plate that was in his hands. He ran to the kitchen in desperation and said to the cook and the kitchen boy, 'Our lives are over, the fortune-teller knows that it was us who stole the ring!' And they all looked at each other with wide frantic eyes.

'But how could he possibly have figured it out?' asked the cook. 'What did he say?'

'Here comes the first one,' the footman said spookily.

They agreed that the cook would take the second course to see what the fortune-teller would say. And as soon as the cook stepped into his room, master Beetle said,

'Here comes the second one.'

These words confirmed their suspicion. The cook became very scared. He put down the plate and ran to the kitchen.

'He definitely knows that we stole the ring. He said to me...'here comes the second one.'

'I wonder what he'll say to me,' the kitchen boy said and he took the third course.

And the cobbler said, 'Here comes the third one.'

When the kitchen boy heard this he became so terrified that he dropped the plate, fell to his knees and confessed to master Beetle that he, the cook and the footman had stolen the queen's ring. And the cook and the footman also ran into the room begging him not to reveal their secret. Each of them would give him two hundred golden pieces.

The cobbler thought about it – he could keep their gold and the king's gold too so he asked for the ring. And when he received it, he pushed it into a piece of bread and threw the piece of bread to the king's turkeys that were pecking below the window. The biggest turkey immediately swallowed it down. Master Beetle ran to the king and told him,

'Your Majesty, you can find the ring in the stomach of your biggest turkey.' At once the biggest turkey was killed, his stomach cut open and wonder of wonders! The ring was revealed! The king took it immediately to the queen and her joy spread throughout the kingdom.

And the king organized a feast in celebration of the great master Beetle. He also gave him six carts loaded with gold. The king lent the cobbler his golden coach and ordered his most noble marshal to accompany master Beetle during his voyage in order to protect the gold for him.

They were on their way to the cobbler's village when a funny thought entered the marshal's mind.

'Wait a minute, you fortune-teller, I'll make fun of you!' He thought. He got off the coach, saw a beetle on the ground and scooped it up. Clasping it in his hands tightly he asked the cobbler,

'Now, fortune-teller, if you are really so wise, tell me what's in the hollow of my hand?'

The cobbler scratched his head and tried to look as though he were thinking deeply. But really he was on thorns. Finally he murmured,

'Now, Beetle, you are in a very tight squeeze.'

'You are right!!' the marshal exclaimed, amazed. 'I really have a beetle in the hollow of my hand. You are the wisest man that I have ever met!' As he opened his hands and a bright green beetle sprung high into the air and hopped away.

During this time they arrived at the cobbler's village. The soldiers who had come along took the lot of gold into the cobbler's house and the people from the whole village came together in admiration. And master Beetle gave away a handful of gold to everyone. But his family, and his best friend, the miller, got most of it. The cobbler also let everyone know that he had finished fortune telling and he had lost his magical book.

And if the magical book hadn't been lost, my tale would have been longer.

Dragon Rose the Most Beautiful Girl in the World

Now children, I am going to tell you a story about Dragon Rose the most beautiful girl in the world and the prince with sparkling eyes.

Once upon a time in the land beyond the Seven Seas, there lived a king. Believe me or not, he ruled over the entire Fable Country. Nobody has ever seen this king smile, not even his queen. He was always sad for not having a child of his own. The king and the queen sighed and grieved for many months and years at their misfortune. They did not know who would inherit their beautiful Fable Country.

Time went by and one day the queen had a dream. In her dream an old man talked to her,

'Do not be sad, Your Majesty. In a year or so you will give birth to a son who will have sparkling eyes and one day he will marry Dragon Rose the most beautiful girl in the world.

When the queen woke up, she was thinking about her dream. She was glad about the prediction but still she could not be happy. She was elated that finally she was going to have a son but she knew that the beautiful Dragon Rose had been kidnapped from her Fairyland country by the Dragon-land's king. Many knights and princes had tried to free her but none of them has come back alive.

One year passed and the old man of her dreams was proven right. The queen gave birth to a boy with sparkling eyes who, even when he was only one day old, was able to stand up on his feet and told his father,

'My dear father, take me to school please, I want to study.'

The king almost fell off his feet when he heard this but he said,

'Of course, I will take you, my dear son. I will have the carriage prepared and I will take you wherever you wish to go.'

Two years went by and the prince had grown up to be a strong young man. He studied at many different schools, travelled the world and when he returned home he told his mother,

'Do you remember, my sweet mother what the old man predicted in your dream?'

And the queen answered very sadly,

'I remember, my dear son, but I wish I had forgotten all about that.'

'Do not be sad, I will search for Dragon Rose, and will bring her back from the Dragons' king,' the prince said.

The queen cried and asked him not to go and not to waste his young life, but all in vain. The prince with sparkling eyes said good bye to his parents and went away to find Dragon Rose. He travelled through many countries and one evening while he walked through a thick forest he saw a bright light in the middle of a puddle. He went closer and looked at it and who do you think he saw? A very beautiful woman was sitting in a tiny golden carriage and as many as six white squirrels tried to pull the tiny carriage but they could not budge it. The prince took the carriage in his hand and lifted it to the edge of the puddle.

'Now, dear prince—I can see it from your face that you are a prince,' said the beautiful woman, 'one good turn deserves another. You should know that I am the fairies' queen. What is your wish?'

'If you are the fairies' queen then your daughter is Dragon Rose, the most beautiful girl in the world. My only wish is to find and marry your daughter!'

The fairies' queen became very sad and started to cry.

'You are right prince. My daughter is Dragon Rose but she is not with me as the Dragons' land's king had kidnapped her. And there is no man who could rescue her. You should know that Dragonls'land's king can bend an iron rod as easily as others knead dough, he can crumble stones as easily as others squeeze sand and he can break tree trunks into small pieces as easily as others tear up yarn. You cannot beat him, don't even think about it.'

'I still want to try,' said the prince, 'if he is as strong as you say I will be stronger and if he is smart I will be smarter.'

'Very well,' said the queen, 'If your are so determined I will give you three golden strands of hair and a string. Strike the three golden hairs with the string and they will turn into a magic steed and the string will become his golden bridle. Mount your steed and he will take you to the bottom of a high mountain. There you will find a spring, take a bath in it and from that moment you are going to be seven times stronger than you are now. Alongside the spring among the bushes you will find a sword but you will only see its tip. Pull this sword out of the earth and fasten it to your belt. Later, when you are tired while fighting with the dragons' king, call your sword:

'Sword! Slide out of the scabbard!' and it will fight for you. But this will still not be enough for you to win. As I told you Dragons'land's king has enormous strength. I will give you three bottles. They contain some magic elixir that will

make you even stronger. If you need them, first drink from the smallest bottle, then from the middle and finally from the largest one. This way perhaps, you can defeat Dragons' land's king.'

When she gave the three bottles to the prince the queen lightly touched the squirrels with her golden whip and then disappeared as quickly as if the earth had swallowed her up. The prince stayed in the middle of the road and took out the three golden strands of hair. He stroke them with the string and, believe me or not, in a twinkle of an eye, they turned into a beautiful steel-grey magic steed. And the string turned into a golden bridle.

The prince leapt on the steed and rode away. By dawn he reached the bottom of the mountain that the fairies' queen mentioned. He took a bath in the spring and in a second he felt seven times stronger than before. He went into the bushes searching for the sword. He soon found it, pulled it out from the earth and fastened it to his waist. He leapt on his horse and was on his way again.

His steel-grey steed flew like the wind or perhaps even faster, so fast that the prince had to close his eyes. But suddenly his steed stopped. The prince opened his eyes, looked around and he saw that he arrived in front of an iron bridge.

'What is the trouble, my sweet horse?'

'Nothing, my dear master, we are here in front of Dragon's land iron bridge. I suggest you have a little rest. As you can see two dragon-snakes guard this bridge and before you step into Dragons' land you will have to kill them first.'

The prince did not want to rest at all. Instead with his horse he jumped on the bridge and in a second he cut the dragon-snakes into small pieces. Then he smartly rode to the centre of Dragons' city. There was the diamond palace of the dragons' king and surrounding the palace was a beautiful meadow where the grass was as fine as silk. And the beautiful Dragon Rose was sitting under a big tree in this meadow. She was very sad.

The prince galloped straight in front of her, jumped off his steed and greeted her warmly,

'Beautiful Dragon Rose I came to rescue you. Do not cry and do not be sad. Your freedom is near!'

But Dragon Rose answered him sadly,

'You came in vain. You should turn back as you cannot save me. I will die here.'

'Is the dragons' king in the palace?' the prince asked.

'No, he is not,' answered Dragon Rose but he will come home by noon and you will be very sorry for being here, my poor prince.'

But the prince said,

'Do not be afraid, my beautiful Dragon Rose, my mother was told that you are going to be my wife and I came for you to fulfill our destiny.'

Before the dragons' king came home Dragon Rose told the prince that there was a big barrel of wine in the cellar of the dragon's king. She thought that the king had gained his strength from this wine as he used to drink it often.

The prince said to Dragon Rose,

'Would you be so kind and bring me a flask of that wine. I would like to try it myself.'

Dragon Rose ran to the cellar and poured a flask of that particular wine and brought it back to the prince. He drank it and really he became much stronger. By this time it was noon and the dragons' king arrived home for lunch. As soon as he rode into his courtyard he saw the prince at once.

'You arrived just at the right time, prince with sparkling eyes. I was waiting for you. I had a dream last night and it told me that you were going to come. Come with me to the clay-meadow, and there we will see who is stronger between us.'

They went to the clay-meadow, where the king broke a big piece of rock into two pieces and he threw one to the prince.

'Now, prince with sparkling eyes! Crush your piece of rock into dust just as I'm doing now and if you can do that we'll know that you are indeed a strong man and a worthy opponent.' And then he promptly crushed his piece of rock into fine dust.

'That is nothing,' the prince said and he did the same.

'I see' the dragons' king said 'you are a strong young man. We can fight now. Just wait a minute. I will run to my cellar and bring my sword.'

'Do not run anywhere,' shouted the prince, 'stay here and we will fight without swords.'

'Fine,' the dragons' king said 'lets fight without swords.' And he grabbed the prince's waist and threw him into the clay knee deep.

But the prince jumped out of the clay right away, grabbed the dragons' king and threw him in the ground waist deep. But the dragons' king jumped out, too and he threw the prince into the clay until only his head was visible. The prince became angry, jumped out, grabbed the dragons' king at his waist and threw him in the clay up to his nose. Now the dragon's king could not jump out anymore. He begged the prince to leave him alive. And the prince said,

'Fine. I do not want your life, I only desire Dragon Rose, the most beautiful girl in the world.'

And the prince was on his way toward the palace but he could not even reach its door yet when the dragons' king climbed out of the clay, ran after him and made him stop,

'Hey, prince, wait a minute! We are not finished yet. I want to fight you again.'

Now the prince took out the three bottles that the fairies' queen gave him and drank all three. He turned to the dragons' king ready to fight. The dragons' king was very confident in his strength as, on his way back from the clay-meadow he rushed to his cellar and drank a lot of wine. He felt he was now invincible.

They faced each other like two bulls and in a second they jumped at each other's throats. They wrestled with one another for hours but neither of them could gain an advantage. The prince felt that he was slowly getting tried. Suddenly he remembered the fairies' queen's words and he shouted out loud,

'Sword out of your scabbard!' and his sword jumped out of its scabbard and cut off the dragons' king head!

You cannot imagine, how happy the beautiful Dragon Rose and the prince were! They were overjoyed. The princess lightly touched the diamond palace with a golden stick and it turned into a diamond apple. She put it in her pocket and they were on their way. They did not stop until the fairies' queen's castle. The young couple married that very same day and held a large wedding banquet. After the celebrations the newlyweds were again on their way and they did not rest until they reached the prince's home. There they held another magnificent wedding, too. And the beautiful Dragon Rose and her brave husband lived happily ever after.

The Poor Man's Rooster

Once upon a time there lived a very poor young man. He had nothing at all, except a little rooster. He became very hungry one day and decided to cook his rooster for dinner.

'Now, rooster,' he said solemnly, 'put some water to boil on the stove so that I can cook you for dinner.'

'Oh, please don't cook me, dear master,' the little rooster begged him, 'I will look for a copper in the rubbish, will buy an egg for you and you can have a supper just like a king.'

And the young man said, 'Fine, but it must be a real egg if you want to save your life.'

The little rooster ran out the door, his tail feathers shaking, but he did not go to the rubbish bin, instead he ran to the forest where he met a rabbit.

'Where are you going, little rooster?'

'I'm going to the well because I heard that if someone takes a bath in its deep water then his hair turn to gold.'

'Wow! Well...can I come too?'

'Of course, but don't come alone, bring your friends.'

The rabbit ran away and soon came back with fifty other rabbits. The little rooster took them to the king's courtyard and reported to the king that his master Prince Rich sends his regards to his Majesty along with fifty rabbits as gifts.

The king was puzzled because he had never heard of this prince. 'Now tell me, little rooster, is your master really so rich?'

'Of course he is,' answered the little rooster, 'he has golden watches in his every pocket.'

The king accepted the presents gladly and gave a piece of gold to the little rooster. Well, you can imagine how happy the little rooster was. He ran back with the piece of gold, bought lots of food and took everything home to his master who was lying on the floor in hunger. The little rooster prepared delicious foods and drinks and gently fed them to the young man.

The food stretched for some time before his master became hungry again and wanted to cook the rooster. The little rooster begged him not to cook him and promised that he would find more food for him. He ran to the forest again and met a wild-hog.

'Where are you going little rooster?'

'I am going to a magic well.'

'Please take me with you,' said the wild-hog.

'Sure, but bring fifty other wild-hogs with you.'

'No problem,' he replied. And sure enough, later that afternoon the little rooster guided fifty wild-hogs to the king's courtyard where they crowded together and were presented as a gift from Prince Rich to the king. The king was surprised but he accepted the nice present and gave a piece of gold to the little rooster. And so that is how the little rooster saved his master's life for a second time and fed him yet again. But not even a week passed by when the young master had eaten all the food that the little rooster had bought, and was hungry again.

This time, the little rooster went to the forest and met a deer there. He told him about the magic well. Of course the deer also wanted to go with him but the little rooster asked him to bring fifty of his friends along. When they had gathered togeth-er, the little rooster led fifty scampering deer to the king's palace. The king began to wonder. He wondered for a while before asking the little rooster,

'Tell me, little rooster, why does your master send me so many presents?'

'He would like to ask for your daughter's hand in marriage, Your Majesty.'

'Really? Then he should come to my palace and introduce himself.'

The little rooster ran home and told his master everything. Oh, how scared the young man became! Poor soul… 'You traitorous rooster!' He said 'How could you do this to me? The king will cut off my head now.'

'Don't be afraid, my dear master, just come with me.'

The poor young man did not have any other choice and he departed with his lit-tle rooster. When they reached the forest, the little rooster told him, 'Wait here, my dear master. I'll go ahead and report to the king that bandits have attacked you and stolen your magnificent outfit, your golden carriage and your horses. Don't worry, the king will send you everything you need.'

And all unfolded just as the little rooster had predicted. He hopped off to the king and was short in breath when he told him that bandits had stolen everything from his master who he had left behind in the forest.

'I certainly am glad that he is safe,' said the king and he ordered his servants to gather the most sophisticated clothes for the little rooster's master and he had his marshal leave in a golden carriage to pick up the young man. The poor soul was na-ked and shivering behind a bush in a thickly shaded part of the forest.

The servants dressed the young master into a golden and velvet outfit and took him to the king's palace. The king introduced him to the princess and because the young man was very handsome, the princess liked him a lot. The king was happy be-cause he knew how rich his future son-in-law was. The princess and the young mas-ter had a splendid wedding that very day; they danced and ate for seven days and seven nights.

When the feast was over, the king asked his son-in-law to take his wife home. Well, the poor soul hadn't expected this! He did not even have a house of his own, how could he take his sophisticated new wife there? Many carriages gathered in front of the king's palace waiting for the newlyweds to depart. Everyone was curious about Prince Rich's palace.

While the young master was lost in his sad thoughts, his little rooster whispered to him, 'Not to worry, my dear master. I will help you. I'm going to go ahead and ar-range everything.'

And so, the little rooster ran ahead and found a herd of cattle on the road. He said to the herdsman, 'Listen, if someone asks you who owns this herd of cattle, tell him it belongs to Prince Rich. And you won't be sorry you did.'

Soon the wedding guests reached the herdsman and they asked him who owned the herd of cattle. He answered 'Prince Rich'. The king glowed with happiness at the wealth of his son-in-law. By this time the little rooster had reached the forest. There was a diamond palace in the forest occupied by twelve thieves. The little rooster ran into the palace and shouted at the thieves to hide themselves quickly because the king was coming with an army and would cut off their heads. The thieves became very frightened and they hid themselves in a haystack. What do you think happened next? The little rooster set light to the haystack and the twelve thieves burned to bits. When the little rooster had finished his task, he ran to the front door of the palace and waited for the king, the young couple and his guests.

In no time at all, the wedding procession arrived at the door and everybody was amazed including Prince Rich! How magnificent, they said about the diamond palace. A second wedding was held in Prince Rich's palace and the king gave half of his kingdom to his son-in-law. When the wedding banquet finished, the young master asked for his rooster and said, 'I have never ever dreamed, my little rooster, that one day I would be such a rich and powerful lord and that the king's daughter would be my wife! I owe everything to you! How can I ever thank you?'

'Hmmmm,' said the little rooster, 'I wish for only two things my dear master. First, neither you, nor any of your relatives will ever eat rooster!'

'It's a promise.'

'And my other request is, I would like to be your treasurer. You know nothing about financial matters.'

'So be it' said the young man, and they both laughed merrily.

And the little rooster made his master even richer than he was already. When the old king died, his son-in-law became the king. And the young king, and his queen and his little rooster lived happily ever after for many years to come.

Talking Grapes, Smiling Apples and Ringing Peaches

Once upon a time there lived a king and his three beautiful daughters. One day the king decided to travel to a neighbouring country where they held a grand fair. So he asked his daughters what they would like him to bring back for them.

The eldest said, 'Please, dear father, bring me a golden dress that shimmers in the sunlight.' The king then turned to her younger daughter who asked him,

'Please, father, bring me a silver dress!'

Finally the king turned to his youngest daughter who was thinking carefully, 'Please bring me, dear father, some talking grapes and smiling apples and ringing peaches.'

The king shook his head, 'Well, I've never ever heard of such things, but if they exist, dear daughter, I will bring them to you.' He smiled warmly at all three of his daughters and then took off in his royal coach. At the fair he bought a golden dress for his eldest daughter and a silver dress for his middle one. He searched and inquired with many merchants about where he could find some talking grapes, smiling apples and ringing peaches, but none of them had ever heard of such things.

The king loved his youngest daughter very much and he became very sad that he couldn't fulfill her wish. He was sitting in his coach and after thinking for some time, he devised a plan. The next day he would announce to the whole country that if anyone could locate some talking grapes, smiling apples and ringing peaches he would give them a sack of gold. Just as he was struck with this perfect plan of action, his carriage suddenly bumped against a tall tree and flew up into the air only to land with a thump, right in the mud. All of the king's horses pulled with all of their might, but they could not budge his coach which was stuck deeply in the mud. So the king sent his servants to fetch help from the village. Many men and women came to help, but no amount of pushing and pulling did any good. They tied a rope around the carriage and the village folk pulled and pulled but in vain.

Suddenly a pig approached the king and told him,

'Give me your youngest daughter in marriage, Your Majesty and I will free your carriage from the mud.'

The king was astonished at this bold request and he broke down into laughter. 'You must be joking pig!' he chortled, 'Well, fine, if you can get my carriage out of the mud then you can have my youngest daughter in marriage. Now, let's see your skill.'

And the pig didn't wait even a second, he put his nose between the front wheels and used all of his strength. And lo and behold! The carriage jumped free and the horses went flying away with the king. Everyone in the village waved as the royal coach went bouncing off towards the palace.

As soon as the king arrived home, he presented the golden dress to his eldest daughter and the silver dress to his younger one. And he then turned sadly towards his youngest daughter,

'My sweet child, why didn't you ask for a beautiful dress too? I couldn't find talking grapes, smiling apples and ringing peaches at the fair, even though I tried very hard.' As he finished what he was saying, a strange noise erupted in the courtyard. The king looked out over the windowsill and there stood the pig grunting loudly.

When the pig saw the king at the window, he grunted to him,

'I've come for your youngest daughter, Your Majesty, send her down and I will take her home in my wheelbarrow.'

'Just wait a second', said the king and he ordered one of his daughter's maids to clothe herself in a golden dress. And he sent her down to the courtyard. But the pig was not fooled,

'This isn't the youngest princess, Your Majesty, send your daughter to me.'

The king panicked. Why did he promise his daughter to this dirty pig! But the king's sadness was nothing compared to the sadness of his youngest daughter when she discovered that her father had made a pawn of her. She sobbed inconsolably and the palace echoed with her sadness.

'Please forgive me, my dear daughter but I cannot change my word to this pig. A king's promise is always set in stone'. But before he let the princess leave, he tried another trick. He ordered the maids to dress the princess in rags. He imagined that the pig might not want her if she were wearing such an ugly outfit. But how wrong he was! When the pig caught sight of the princess he nearly burst with joy. He picked her up and nestled her in the wheelbarrow and said, 'Don't cry sweet princess, I will take good care of you!'

But the princess cried throughout the whole journey. And she became even more upset when the pig stopped in front of a pigsty which was to be her new home. The pig lifted her up and gently lay her down on the straw. Poor soul, she was so tired she fell asleep on the spot.

And she slept until the following day. The next morning she awoke not knowing where she was, but she remembered everything that had happened the day before. When she rolled over and raised her lids she discovered that she was lying on a golden canapé bed inside a dazzling beautiful palace. As soon as she stirred, maids ran to her bedside asking what she would like. And they brought her magnificent dresses from which she chose an embroidered one made of silk. As soon as she was dressed, she was led into the next room where a very handsome young man was sitting at a table. When he saw the princess, he jumped to his feet, took her by the hand and let her to the table.

'Have a sit, beautiful princess,' he said, 'everything belongs to you here, including me.'

'Who are you?' the astonished princess asked.

'I will tell you later, but first please come with me into my garden.'

And they walked arm in arm into the garden. As soon as they arrived there, the princess saw a vine-stock along the road and its bunch of grapes asked her,

'Pick me, pick me beautiful princess!'

'These are the talking grapes,' the young man said.

They walked further and soon they came across a beautiful apple tree. And the red apples of the tree were smiling at the princess.

'See,' the young man said, 'these are the smiling apples.'

They walked a short distance again when suddenly the whole garden echoed a lovely tinkling sound. The princess looked in every direction and asked her companion,

'What makes that nice sound?'

'Look at that peach tree,' the young man said, 'it has ringing peaches.'

You can imagine how happy the princess became when she realized that the garden had talking grapes, smiling apples and ringing peaches! She cried and laughed in her joy.

'See,' the young man said, 'my garden has all those fruits, you wished for. Would you like to stay here with me and be my wife?'

And the princess jumped into the young man's arms and happily said 'yes'. Then the young man explained his story to the princess. He had been a prince, he said but a wicked witch wanted him to marry her daughter. When he did not obey her, the witch turned him into a pig. And she cursed him that he would stay a pig unless a girl wished for some talking grapes, smiling apples and ringing peaches.

'So I can thank you that I can be a prince again' he said to the princess.

Their happiness was beyond words. They let the princess' father know the very day about what happened, and invited him along with his two daughters and his court for their wedding. And the following day a splendid wedding was held with great merry-making. They both lived happily ever after for many years to come and enjoyed their talking grapes, smiling apples and ringing peaches in their magical garden.

The Pelican

Once upon a time, beyond the seven seas and seven countries, there lived an old king with one smiling eye and one crying eye. No one knew the reason and everyone wondered why both of his eyes wouldn't be smiling when he had a very good reason to be happy. His daughter was so beautiful that no one else in the whole world could hold a candle to her. What could be bothering the king the people wondered. How could he be sad when all the princes from the neighbouring countries would love to come to his court to compete for the princess' hand? After all he did not have to worry that his daughter would not find a suitable husband. The princess herself worried about her father and one day she asked him,

'Father, please tell me, why is one of your eyes is smiling and the other is crying?'

The King touched the princess' hand and sighed deeply,

'Oh, my dear daughter, many people have asked me that question, but I have never talked about it to anyone. And why should I? It wouldn't do me any good.'

'But please tell me so at least I will understand.' The princess said. And she asked him so genuinely that finally the old king told her,

'Let me tell you why one of my eyes is crying.' The king drew a deep breath and began. 'When I was young, I had a lovely singing pelican and when she sang I would forget about all of my troubles. Somebody stole her from me and although I looked for her everywhere I could imagine, she was never found. Ever since one of my eyes cries. However my other eye smiles as I have seen many beautiful girls during my voyages but nobody has come close to your radiance.

And the princess replied,

'If that is why you are sad then I will not marry anyone until your pelican is found! You can announce that if any prince wishes to marry me, first he must find your pelican. Until then I do not wish to see any of them!'

The old King tried to talk his daughter out of her decision but she had made up her mind. He feared that she may wait a long time before the pelican was found. The princess herself made the announcement of her promise to marry only the man who returns her father's singing pelican to the palace.

You can imagine the response! Over a hundred princes took to the paths leading away from the palace grounds. They travelled through all the countries of the world and every one of them came back empty handed. They could not find the beautiful singing pelican.

'You see, my dear daughter,' the king said, 'You will come to regret your decision for you'll become an old woman before the pelican is found.'

The princess shrugged her shoulders, 'Father you should think more optimistically. If finding your pelican is what will make you happy then it will be found.' The old king became very sad when he heard this and both of his eyes began crying. He was afraid that his daughter would never marry and he was very sorry that he told his daughter about the pelican.

There was a very kind young nobleman in the king's court who heard of the king's sorrow and the princess' wish. He asked the cook to bake a scone especially for him. When the cook gave it to him he silently left the city, without anyone knowing. After a few days' journey he arrived at a big forest. At the edge of the forest an old beggar appeared asking him, in the name of Peace, for a piece of bread. The young nobleman handed him half his scone.

'You can thank your lucky stars that you were generous to me.' The old beggar said. 'I know your heart's desire. Many princes on shining horses rode this way before you and I asked every one of them for a piece of bread but they all ignored me and rode away. I watched them return along this same road empty handed.' The old man shook his head. 'Well, one good turn deserves another, my son. Listen to me carefully.

The king's pelican lives beyond the seven seas and even if you had three lives it still wouldn't be enough time to get there. You need a horse who drank dragon milk as a baby. Go through this forest and when you reach its border you will find an old witch's house.' He pointed over his shoulder and the young man continued to listen carefully. 'Offer yourself as a servant. When you spend time with her, a year lasts three days but nobody has ever been able to serve her for that long.'

The old man looked at him carefully, 'You scared?' The young man's eyes were wide, but he shook his head vigorously. The old man continued to explain how it was the servant's responsibility to guard the witch's two horses and make sure that they didn't escape. Each evening he would have to take them home, but the pair of horses would hide themselves so cleverly – sometimes under the earth or beneath the sea or even above the clouds – that none of the servants could find them. They would only come home once the three days had passed and the old witch had cut her servant's head off!

'But do not be afraid my son. Take this whistle. It has three holes. If you blow into the first hole, the king of the butterflies will appear and be ready to serve you. If you blow into the second hole, the king of the fish will appear and if you blow into the third hole, the king of the mice will arrive. Each will find where the horses are hiding. When you have served three days, the old witch will offer you treasures beyond your wildest dreams, but do not accept them. Instead, ask for the filly which is hidden underneath the dunghill. Dig up this filly and carry her round your neck and do not stop until you reach the bridge at the edge of the village. Wash the filly under the bridge in the river.'

The young man thanked the old man for the whistle and good advice. He bid him good-bye and was on his way. By the evening he arrived at another forest in which he found the old witch's house. She opened the door before he had a chance to knock.

'What are you up to my son?'

'Looking for work, my dear lady.'

'Very well, my son,' said the witch, 'you've come to the right place and at an auspicious hour. Three days make a year if you stay with me and you'll have to look after my two horses. But if you let them run away you'll lose your head.'

'Your horses are safe with me.'

'We'll see,' murmured the old witch to herself.

She prepared a tasty supper for the lad, with plenty of wine, but she sprinkled some sleeping powder into his wineglass. After the meal she lead him to the stable and asked him to take the horses to the silky-meadow and have them back by the morning.

So the young man fitted the horses with their bridles and took them to the silky-meadow as the witch had instructed. He let them run free and lay down on the grass for a rest but soon enough he had fallen asleep. The sun was high in the sky when he woke up. He looked all around but he could not see the horses.

He fished the whistle out of his pocket and blew into the first hole. In a second the butterflies' king appeared before him,

'What is your wish sweet master?'

'Find my horses please!'

'If they are in the air, do not worry, I will find them and bring them back. When they will be back, you just hit their heads with a bridle.'

And the butterflies' king flew away. He called together all the butterflies and asked them to look for the two horses. Not an hour had passed when the young man saw an army of butterflies chasing two griffins toward the silky meadow. When the griffins reached the ground the young man, remembering the butterflies' king's advice, hit the two griffins' heads with a bridle. At that moment the two griffins turned into two horses. He put the bridles on their backs and rode home.

The old witch smiled wryly when she saw the young man returning with the two horses and she praised him for a job well done. She covered her table with delicious food and while the lad was eating she crept out the back door and made her way to the stable. She was so furious with her horses for not hiding in a better spot that she hit them with her shovel! She hit them so hard that they fell to the floor.

On the second evening the old witch again gave the young man a tasty supper but this time she put even more sleeping powder in his wine. He became so sleepy that he did not even reach the meadow when he fell from his horse and did not wake up until the next morning. As you might guess he could not find his horses. But he remained calm and blew into his whistle's second hole. The fish's king appeared in front of him.

And the young man told him his problem.

'Do not worry about your horses,' said the fish's king, 'if they are in my country, you can be sure I will find them.'

And, sure enough, within an hour a huge pike appeared in the silky meadow. Using a sword-fish the fish's king slit open the pike's belly and behold…! Two golden fish fell out! The young man gently stroked the two little gold fish with a bridle and in a blink the two little gold fish turned into the two lost horses and he rode them home.

Seeing her horses again, the old witch smiled and praised the young man for a job well done. But while he ate his lunch the witch went to the stable and hit her horses so hard that they fell flat on the floor again. The third evening the old witch put much more sleeping powder into the young man's wine and gave him three thick pillows to sleep better. He did not need the pillows though because he fell asleep right away and did not wake up until noon the next day. When he woke he knew that the two horses were gone. He did not even look for them, instead he blew into the third hole of his whistle and the Mouse King appeared before him.

'What is your wish my master?'

'Find my horses please!'

'Don't worry. If they are underground then I will find them.'

And the Mouse King ordered his servants to look in every underground nook. In a few minutes they found two rats and they escorted them to the young man. He stroked them lightly with his bridle and in a flash they turned back into two horses. He put their bridles on and rode home for the third time.

'I have to tell you, my son,' the old witch said, when the young man arrived safely home with the horses, 'that I've never had such an outstanding servant as you. You have served me well and I am in your debt. Here are three keys. The largest one opens my cellar door where you will find barrels full of gold and silver. Take as many coins as you wish and as much as you can carry. The middle keys opens my dressing room. There are clothes sewn with gold, diamonds and pearls. Choose the most beautiful outfit for yourself. The smallest key is for my stable. You can choose any one of my fillies.'

But the young man remembered the old man's advice and said,

'My dear lady, I don't want any of your gold, your clothing or your fillies. I only want the horse that is buried under your dunghill.'

'You are a fool, my son,' the old witch said, 'What would you do with that dirty horse?'

'Never mind, just give me a spade so I can dig.'

The witch realized that she had lost her power over the young man and that she couldn't get her way with him so she gave him her smallest spade and left him to his search in the dunghill. He dug for seven days and seven nights and behold he finally found the filly. He lifted her tenderly to his shoulders and made his way to the river by the bridge where he gently scrubbed her clean. And what do you think happened when the filly was clean and she walked out to the shore? She turned into a magnificent steed! She even had a bridle with diamond studs and a saddle of brilliant shining gold and silver.

'Now, dear master, jump on my back and let's see how well you can ride.'

Within moments they were flying in the air among the highest clouds. But she didn't stop! The young man sat firmly on her back as if he were pinned there. They flew all the way to the moon. From the moon to the sun and from the sun to the spot where the Milky Way starts and then they began to descend and the young man soon found himself back at the bridge in the village.

The magical steed neighed, 'You were brave, my master. Now I will take you to the Seven Seas. There is a tree on one side of the sea and another tree on the other side. These two trees lean against each other twice a year. At the beginning of the spring and at the end of the summer they touch each other for a short time to form a bridge. So you can walk from one side of the sea to the other. And that is what you should do. When you reach the other side of the Seven Seas continue to walk by foot and ask everyone you meet about the pelican. If you ever need me just blow into the three holes of your whistle and I will be there.'

As the steed said these words, she jumped into the air and flew over the forests and seas and meadows. She flew as fast as a thought for seven days and seven nights before reaching the shore of the Seven Seas.

'Here we are, my little master, take the bridle from my mouth and go.'

The young man looked towards the shore where, just as his steed had said, there was a tree leaning far across the sea. The young man ran and jumped onto it and ran like the wind across its trunk. Soon he was on the other side and he jumped down. Just in time too! As soon as he landed on the ground, the two trees began to straighten.

And the young man walked on and soon saw a golden forest in the distance. Upon reaching the forest's edge he found a little house. A hundred year old woman lived there. The young man greeted her,

'Good evening lady.'

'Good evening to you too, my son. Do tell me, what has brought you here?'

'I am looking for the beautiful singing pelican. Have you ever heard of such a bird?'

'Oh, yes I have heard about her, but I've never seen her. I would love to hear her sing. They say that those who listen to her song will become young again. I suggest you visit my mother. She lives near the silver forest and knows more about the pelican than I do.'

And so the young man walked over sunny hills and through marshy valleys until he reached the silver forest. When he met the old woman he asked her about the pelican.

'I have heard about her my son, and I know that the fairies keep her in a golden cage. They guard her day and night and you can never get near. I suggest that you visit my mother. She lives in the brass forest and knows more about the pelican than me.'

She showed the young man the way and he reached the brass forest where the old woman's mother lived.

'Good evening, my son. You are looking for the beautiful singing pelican aren't you?'

'Indeed, my lady.'

'And my daughter told you that the fairies put her in a golden cage. That was true...until today. This morning when the fairies opened the cage door to feed her the pelican flew away. And I am the only one who knows where she is.'

'Oh my dear lady, please tell me! I would forever be in your debt. This beautiful singing pelican belongs to my king. And one of his eyes is always crying for this pelican.'

'I know she was your king's pelican, my son and I will tell you how to find her. Listen carefully. The pelican flew to the iron forest and it's legs got stuck in the branches of a tree that touches the sky and she could not free herself. Someone must climb that tree to free her. But I don't believe that anyone can.'

The young man felt like crying at her last words. He did not know what to do when he remembered his whistle! He took it out and blew into its three holes. Suddenly a strong wind blew across the sky and his magic steed appeared in front of him.

'What is your trouble, my dear master?'

And the young man explained everything to her.

'Sit on my back and hold onto my mane. Do not look right or left, only look up. I will take you to that tree. When my head reaches the clouds, grab onto the two branches where the pelican's legs are stuck. Pull the branches apart , catch the pelican and put her into your overcoat.'

They flew directly to the iron forest where they found the tree whose top reached the sky. When the steed's head touched the clouds the young man quickly grabbed onto two branches of the enormous tree and pulled them apart. As the wondrous pelican began to fall he caught her and put her in his overcoat.

And what do you think happened next? Wonder of wonders! As soon as the pelican was safely in the young man's overcoat, she started to sing and the earth and the sky echoed her song.

Hearing this the steed warned his young master, 'Hold onto me tightly my dear master, otherwise you will fall down.' The steed had warned him at just the right moment. The young man was so enthralled listening to the pelican's song that he almost fell from his steed's back.

But soon enough, they were safely on their way. The young man and the magical steed had several people to visit on their journey home. The three old women who earlier helped the young man to find the pelican became young women again when they listened to the pelican's song.

One week went by and the young man finally arrived at his city. He took out the beautiful singing pelican and told her, 'Sing, sing, beautiful pelican!'

And she started to sing. Everybody ran to the streets including the king himself and when the king listened to her song he too became young again. He looked as if he were his own daughter's brother!

And everybody celebrated the young nobleman as their hero. The king gave him half of his country and his daughter's hand in marriage. And they all lived happily ever after with the pelican. Maybe, one day, long after the day of the king and his beautiful daughter, the beautiful singing pelican will be your guest.

The Princess' Shoes

Once upon a time, a very long time ago, far beyond the end of the world, there lived a king and his beautiful daughter. This princess was as beautiful as a clear night sky, however, she was also very conceited and while the palace was full of interesting and lively princes none of them was good enough for her. She only laughed and made fun of them, teased and embarrassed them. There was, however, one among them who she fancied a little and he was made fun of most of all!

With each passing day the princess' beauty grew and she continued to tease her suitors and she promised marriage to none. In time the princes became broken-hearted and they left the palace one after the other. It happened one day that two fleas jumped onto the princess' palms. In a second flat she pressed her palms together and put the two fleas into a pot full of fat. In one year the two fleas became so big in the pot that their skins could be used to make a pair of shoes!

The princess called for the butcher to skin the fleas. So he skinned the fleas and the shoe-maker made a beautiful pair of shoes from their skins for the princess. And the princess announced that she would marry the man who discovered the animal skin of which her shoes were made.

News of the princess' challenge travelled fast. You can imagine how crowded the king's palace became again. Princes, knights and young noble men flooded from every direction and they spent days and days thinking and discussing and reading

animal skin manuals without coming close guessing the secret of the princess' shoes. Some exhausted themselves recounting long lists of rare skins from ancient biology texts but no one found the correct answer!

The prince whom the princess had teased the most, dressed up as a beggar. He didn't want to be recognized by anyone because he had a secret idea. He hid himself in the princess' bedroom hoping that the princess would talk about her shoes to her chambermaid!

By the evening when the princess came to her room, she was in a very good mood. She laughed loudly and told her chambermaid about the many foolish answers she had heard that day.

'You will see,' she said to her chambermaid 'none of those fools will find out that my shoes were made from fleas' skin!'

'You are right, Your Majestic princess,' the chambermaid said, 'I doubt that any are clever enough.'

A smile grew on the hiding prince's lips. He nearly fell from his hiding spot. The next day he wore his beggar cloths and joined the throng of young men who were deep in thought over the princess' mysterious shoes. When it was his turn, the clever prince dressed in beggar's clothes spoke loudly and clearly, 'Majestic princess, your shoes were made from fleas' skin!'

The princess became as pale as chalk and she began to tremble like an aspen-leaf.

'It is true, you are right, beggar. And now I'll have to be your wife.'

Two sets of arms reached out as her knees turned to jelly. However, the proud princess soon regained her great strength and the life flooded back into her cheeks. She quickly forgot her embarrassment and looked directly into the eyes of the bedraggled beggar and said 'Very well, clever man, we shall marry however don't think that you can push me around.'

'As you wish, dear lady.' He said.

And they got married right there on the spot. After the wedding the prince in beggar cloths said,

'Very well, take off your delicately embroidered silk dress, my beautiful wife and dress in these clothes. We suit each other this way.' He held up a brown shapeless dress and a handkerchief to tie back her hair.

And so the conceited princess dressed in beggar cloths and accompanied her husband to the border of the village where he had a little thatched house. Together they begged from dawn to dusk and made a fire every evening over which to cook their suppers.

One day a serviceman came to the little house. Loudly he called,

'You, beggar woman pick yourself up and go to work in the prince's field!'

Oh, poor soul. She began to cry but she could not do anything and so she went on her way. As soon as she was out of sight, her husband made his way to his palace and changed his beggar cloths into a golden and velvet outfit. Then he went to his field to find his servants including his own wife.

He praised every one of his labourers except his wife. Supper time came and a very strange thing happened. All of the workers received a silver spoon, a silver fork and a silver knife instead of the usual wooden cutlery. And the prince had a silver spoon secretly put into the beggar woman's pocket. You can imagine the uproar that followed the dinner when the servants discovered that one silver spoon was missing!

They searched everywhere until finally one silver spoon was found in the beggar woman's pocket. She swore she did not steal it but nobody believed in her. The poor soul cried and cried when the prince finally realised that the lesson was too harsh. Tenderly he took the hand of the beggar woman, led her to his palace and said,

'Please, do not cry anymore, my dear wife. Don't you recognize me? I am your husband! Put on your fairest dress. Then we will match!' But the princess was stunned. She stared at him, her eyes wild and suspicious. The prince laughed,

'Look at me carefully and you will see that I am the beggar that you married.'

He told her that he was madly in love with her when they first met but that she had been so mean and had humiliated him so much that he decided to trick her to find out what kind of skin her shoes were.

The newly humbled princess threw her arms around the lovely prince and they made peace with one another. And they held a splendid wedding characterized by great merriment. And they both lived happily for many years to come.

The Magic Stick

A long time ago in a village far away lived a poor logger. He was poorer even than a church mouse. He worked very hard cutting the trees in the forest from dawn until late evening yet he hardly had anything to eat for lunch or supper. He often had only some dry bread and water.

Once while he was sitting under a tree having his lunch an old man approached him and asked for a piece of bread.

'With pleasure,' the poor logger said, 'I can see that you are even poorer than I am.' And he broke his loaf of bread in half and gave it to the old man.

'One good turn deserves another one,' the old man said. 'You should know, that I reward good, generous people and punish those who are selfish. Since you offered me a piece of your bread, you deserve something in return.'

'What could I possibly get from this old man?' the logger thought. Just then the old man pulled a table-cloth from his satchel and said,

'I give you this magic table-cloth, poor logger. Next time when you feel hungry you only have to say to the table-cloth: "Give me some food and drink"! And as you will see you will have more than enough.'

The poor logger thanked the old man, said good-bye to him and started to go home. But before he reached his house he became very hungry. There was a tavern nearby. He went in as he wanted to try out his new magic table-cloth. He sat down at a table, took out the table-cloth and said, 'Give me food and drink!'

And can you imagine what happened? In a twinkling of an eye the table-cloth was covered with delicious hot and cold food, tasty meats and some wonderful bottles of wine. The tavern-keeper ran to the poor logger, clapped his hands in amazement and asked him,

'Where did you find this magic table-cloth, poor logger?' And the poor logger told him the whole story.

The tavern-keeper and his wife immediately wanted to be his friends. They sat down beside him and joined him in the meal. When they finished they asked him to stay for the night. They waited until he was asleep and then they took away his magic table-cloth and replaced it with an ordinary one.

In the morning the poor logger departed for his home and did not stop until he reached his house. He was very happy as he told his wife,

94

'My dear wife, we are not poor anymore. An old man gave me a magic table-cloth and I only have to ask and it gives me lots of delicious food and drinks. So much food that the whole village would have enough to eat.'

'You are mad, my dear husband,' said his wife.

'If you don't believe me, I will show you!' And he took out the table-cloth and ordered,

'Give me food and drink!'

But it was all in vain—nothing had happened.

'That was a cruel joke to play on me,' his wife said. 'You should go back to the forest and cut some trees. We will then have some money for food at least.'

'I don't know what happened,' the poor man said, 'this table-cloth gave me food and drinks earlier.' He was very upset and tried to order the table-cloth again and again but it was all in vain. He never thought that the tavern-keeper and his wife had exchanged his magic table-cloth for an ordinary one.

He went back to the forest to cut some trees but all the while he was very sad. At noon he took a break, sat down under a tree and took out a piece of dry bread to eat. While he was eating the old man whom he met earlier and who gave him the magic table-cloth appeared and again asked him for a piece of bread.

'With pleasure,' the poor logger said, 'although your table-cloth has given me a lot of grief. It gave me food and drink only once, but never again!'

'If it did not give you food and drink then it was a different table-cloth.' The old man said. 'Someone must have replaced it. But never mind. This time I will give you a lamb. You just have to ask him, 'Dance, my little lamb' and gold pieces will fall from his wool like water drops in a shower. But take good care of him, don't let anybody steal it.'

Then the old man pulled out a white, cuddly little lamb from his satchel. He gave it to the logger and disappeared as if the earth had swallowed him. The poor logger was very happy with his new gift. He stopped his work and started to walk back home. As it happened he went to the same tavern again and when he met the tavern-keeper and his wife he proudly started to boast about his lamb.

'Let us see,' said the tavern-keeper and his wife 'if it is really true.' And the logger ordered the little lamb,

'Dance my little lamb, dance.' And wonder of wonders, the lamb started to dance and dozens of gold coins fell from his wool like shower.

'Pick them up quickly,' he told the tavern-keeper and his wife. 'You can keep those few gold coins for yourselves. From now on I can have a lot of money whenever I want!'

But the tavern-keeper and his wife were not satisfied with the few gold pieces. They wanted a lot more! So when the logger fell asleep later in the evening, they stole his magic lamb and placed a similar looking one in its place. As you can imagine when the poor logger arrived home and asked the little lamb to dance it was all in vain. He did not dance and there were no gold coins.

The poor man was devastated and his wife was crying—she was afraid that her husband had finally lost his mind. The logger went back to the forest but he could not work, he was so upset. During lunch time he sat under a trec and took out his bread but could not eat as he was so sad. Suddenly the same old man appeared in front of him but this time he did not asked him for a piece of bread.

He asked him

'You are sad, aren't you, poor logger? Your lamb was stolen wasn't it? You should know that the tavern-keeper and his wife had stolen your magic table- cloth and your magic lamb. But don't be sad. I will help you once again but for the last time. Take this stick, go to the tavern and tell the stick: 'Hit them hard stick! And the stick will hit the tavern-keeper and his wife until they will give you back your magic table-cloth and your magic lamb. But this time take very good care of this stick. It can even hit a whole army if you ask!' Saying this the old man disappeared. And the poor logger went directly to the tavern carrying the stick with him.

When he arrived, he first asked the tavern-keeper and his wife to give him back his magic table-cloth and the lamb but they denied they ever took them from him. So the logger ordered his stick,

'Hit them hard stick!' And the tavern-keeper and his wife got a real beating! The stick hit their heads and backs until they lay down on the floor in pain. Finally they could not stand it any more and they gave back the magic table-cloth and the lamb to the logger.

You can imagine how happy the poor logger was! He ran home quickly with the table-cloth and the lamb to show them to his wife. As soon as he arrived, he ordered the magic table-cloth, 'Give me food and drink!' And in a twinkling of an eye the table-cloth was covered with delicious food and different kind of wines. People came from the whole village to eat and drink and there was more than enough food and drink for everyone.

And the poor logger asked his magic lamb, 'Dance, my little lamb, dance!' And he started to dance and he showered them with gold coins. The news of the magic table-cloth and the lamb spread like fire throughout the whole country. Princes, barons, rich and poor came to see for themselves. Finally the king himself came. And the king told the logger,

'I heard the news about your magic table-cloth and the magic lamb. I want to see if the news is true. But if it is a lie I will have your head cut off.'

The poor logger was not scared, he asked his table-cloth, 'Give me food and drink!' And in a second the magic table-cloth was covered with the best foods and drinks. The king ate as much as he could.

"Now I want to see the lamb.' Ordered the king.

'Dance, my little lamb, dance!' the logger asked his magic lamb. And he began to dance and showered everyone with gold pieces.

'Very well,' the king said, 'I demand that you hand over the table-cloth and the lamb. I want to have them in my palace by tomorrow lunch time.'

The poor soul now became very scared. If he does not obey, the king certainly cuts his head off. Finally he decided to reject the king's demand. He will not take his treasures to the king and if someone were to come for them he would ask for his stick's help.

The next day before noon the king's Marshall arrived at his house with twelve soldiers and ordered him to come with them and bring his magic table-cloth and his lamb.

The logger said

'I'm coming, coming just wait a second!' Then he ordered his stick,

'Hit them hard, stick!'

And the stick started to hit the Marshall and the soldiers so hard that they could hardly escape. They all ran away as fast as they could and told the king what happened. And the king became very angry with the poor logger. He collected his army and he personally took charge as they marched against the logger. When the king and his army arrived at the poor logger's house the logger saw them and ordered his stick,

'Hit them hard, stick!'

And the stick hit the king's head so hard that he immediately fell off his horse and died on the spot. When the soldiers realized that their king was dead, they stopped their fight and held a meeting to discuss the logger's fate. And can you imagine what happened? They chose the poor logger as their new king! And it happened just like that. The poor logger became a king and everybody loved him in his country. He and his wife lived happily ever after for many years to come.

The Three Young Noble Men

There was once a noble man who had three handsome sons. The three sons decided one day to leave their childhood home and try their luck in the world. Taking up their swords, they said good-bye to their father who watched their shadows grow small before they disappeared over the rolling hills that surrounded their small village. In the evening the three young men arrived at a big forest where they built a fire beneath a tree to lay down for the night.

Their eyelids had not quite closed when an old woman approached asking to let her lie down beside their fire.

'Please rest your head, old woman,' said the eldest brother, and they chatted for a short while before falling asleep. When they awoke in the morning, the old woman thanked the brothers for the accommodation and she gave a small purse to the eldest brother,

'Keep this purse, my son and take good care of it, and you'll find that money never disappears.'

The three brothers were pleased at having such good luck on their first day. They thanked the kind woman for the gift and departed. By the evening they arrived at a wide river. They couldn't go any further so they lay down on the river-bank. The same old woman came again and asking to stay with them for the night. In the morning when they were about to depart, the old woman gave the middle brother a hat. She said,

'Take care of this hat, my son. This is a magical hat. Once it's on your head you'll become invisible.'

The three brothers thanked her very much for the second mysterious gift and continued on their journey. Three days later they arrived at a big city. The eldest brother said,

'Let's see whether my little purse gives us any money. If it does, we can buy our own house to sleep in.'

As he opened the purse his eyes grew wide as he found that it was full of silver and gold coins! Immediately the brothers bought a most beautiful house and ate a nice supper and prepared for bed.

As soon as their heads touched their pillows the old woman knocked upon the door asking for a warm place to rest for the night. Of course they immediately invited

99

her inside and thanked her very much for their good fortune. They made a warm bed for her by the wood stove and bid her sweat dreams. When they woke up the next morning, they discussed what to do; should they stay in the city or travel further? The youngest brother said,

'Let's continue on. Nobody knows how brave we are yet.'

The old woman chimed in,

'Go away and you will have even more luck. Take this golden stick, my son,' she said to the youngest brother, 'and if you ever run into trouble, just flick it and an army will come to your help.' The brothers did not have a chance to thank the old woman for her good will and kindness because she disappeared right before their startled eyes.

And so the brothers travelled further. On the following day they arrived at another big city which was ruled by the Black King. He had such a beautiful daughter that her charm and beauty was spoken of for miles. The princess announced that she would only marry the young man who was able to outplay her at dice. However she also announced that if her suitor was not successful then his head would be cut off. This announcement did not scare away the many princes, counts, barons and noble men who came to the palace to try their luck. But they paid a very high price for their bravery. The princess outplayed every one of them in dice. Every last one lost his head!

The three brothers heard about the princess and decided to try their luck at her game. First the eldest brother went to the palace and reported to the king that he would like to marry his daughter.

'Very well, my son,' the king said, 'but do you know that ninety-nine young men have lost their lives for that very reason?'

'I still would like to try,' he said and he was escorted to the princess' room.

The princess sat at her table alone playing with some dice. The young man's entrance surprised her and one of the die fell through her fingers and struck the marble floor. The oldest brother thought that the princess looked very lovely. He sat down on the other side of the table and they began to play. It was morning when they started and they were still playing late into the afternoon and the princess was the winner every time. But she could not win all of his money of the young man because he had his magic purse and was able to pay his debt every time.

'I can see,' she said, 'we will be here for a long time before I win all of your money. Give me your purse and I will marry you.'

And the eldest brother believed her words and gave the magic purse to the princess. As soon as she had it she called,

'Guards, throw this man out of my room!'

And the guards threw him onto the streets where his younger brothers found him later that evening, bruised and struck with sadness.

'What happened, dear brother? Why won't you speak?' they asked. When he found his voice he told them how the princess had tricked him.

'It's my turn now,' the middle brother said, 'I will try my luck.'

The middle brother climbed up the palace wall and into the princess' chambers.

'Majestic Princess,' he said, startling her 'I've come to retrieve my brother's purse.'

'Who do you think you are?' The princess screamed angrily. 'Guards, throw this man out!'

But the young man placed his magic hat on his head and became invisible. When the guards finally left after looking for him in every corner of the palace, the young man took off his hat and stood before the princess. So she realized that the hat had special powers. She began to gently caress the young man face and asked him to let her try the hat on, just for a moment... and the foolish young man let her do it. The princess immediately called the guards to throw him out.

Sadly he returned to his brothers and told them what had happened. No sooner had the story been told than the youngest brother announced boldly,

'I will bring back both the purse and the hat.' And he went to the palace. In front of it he flicked his golden stick three times and in a flash three armies stood behind him. His modest cloth became a gold and velvet shining outfit. He went directly to the princess' room. The king and his court were all there. The young man said loudly.

'Majestic Princess, please give back my brothers' purse and hat.'

Of course the king called for the guards to throw out the young man. But his anger quickly changed to fear when the young man's armies opened fire upon his palace.

'Don't be angry with me, my son. Please send away your soldiers, I would rather give you my daughter and half of my kingdom.'

The young man leaned out of the window and flicked his golden stick three times.

His armies suddenly disappeared as if the earth had swallowed them up along with his gold and velvet shining clothing and he stood there in his modest outfit. But he was holding his golden stick. And the princess approached him.

'What a beautiful golden stick you have. Can I hold it for a second?'

The young man shook his head.

'I will be your wife soon.' The princess said. 'You heard that my father promised my hand to you. Please let me touch your golden stick just for a second.'

And the young man gave her the golden stick. And his fate was the same as his brothers. The king called the guards and they threw him out. And the poor youngest brother was so ashamed of himself that he did not dare to go back to his brothers.

He went on his way without any direction and in the evening he found himself wandering through a dark forest. He lay down under a tree and fell asleep. In his dream he saw the old woman who gave him the golden stick and gave his brothers the purse and the hat. She said to him,

'You and your brothers have been clumsy and foolish, my son but I will help you once more. There is a magic spring in this forest and there is an apple tree beside the spring. Fill up your flask, my son from the water of the magic spring and tear two apples from the tree but you must not drink from the water of the spring and must not take a bite of the apples. Put on a peasant cloth to hide your identity and take the two apples to the king's palace. The king will buy your apples as they will be the most beautiful that he has ever seen. When the king, the queen and their daughter eat the apples they will all lose their minds! And the best doctors won't be able to cure them. That's when you put on doctor's cloth and report to the majordomo. One drop of water from the magic spring will be enough to cure them.'

When the young man woke up the next morning this dream filled his head. Could it be true? The magic spring was very close to the tree under which he had spent the night. Beside this magic spring there was an apple tree with two shiny red apples hanging from a branch. He filled his flask with water from the magic spring and pulled the two apples from the tree. He changed into a peasant's outfit and then made his way to the king's palace.

As he had hoped the king bought the two apples. The palace cook cut them into slices and then the king, the queen and the princess ate until only the seeds were left. And they all lost their mind! As soon as the servants realized that something was very wrong with the royal family, the most famous doctors were called from every corner of the country to cure them but none of them was successful. Then the youngest brother arrived wearing his doctor's cloth and declaring that he could cure their illness that very day.

The bold young doctor put one drop of magic spring water in the king's mouth and as soon as he had swallowed it, his eyes cleared and he regained his sanity! Everyone gasped. He then gave one magic drop to the queen. She became healthy too. But the youngest brother did not give the magic drop to the princess. Everyone laughed as the poor soul spoke such silly nonsense. The king and the queen begged the doctor to cure their daughter who was becoming more and more of an embarrassment as each minute passed.

'Very well,' the youngest brother said, 'In fact I am not a doctor but the youngest of the three brothers whose treasures your daughter stole from us. Give your daughter's hand in marriage to me and return the purse, the hat and the golden stick and then I will cure her.'

The king and the queen had no choice—they promised the princess' hand to the young lad and gave back all that had been taken.

Then the young man gave the princess a drop of water from the magic spring. Upon recovery she immediately recognized the youngest brother. She laughed heartily and said,

'You were always the one I was fond of.'

'Would you marry me then, beautiful princess?' he asked.

'Yes, I would' she said.

And their wedding was splendid. The Black King gave his whole kingdom to the youngest brother. The two older brothers were also invited and they met two beautiful and kind court ladies who they married. And everybody lived happily ever after.

The Single Rosemary

There once lived a young king who was loved very much by his subjects. Their only worry was that the king was still a bachelor. 'What would happen to their country if the king should die without producing an heir?' People talked and talked about this until everyone in the kingdom became concerned. It came to seem that the fate of their country depended upon the king finding a suitable bride.

Of course the young king wanted to marry very badly and he travelled through many countries but without any luck. Then he remembered an old hunter who lived in his forest and was known for his wisdom. The king decided to seek his advice. After some time searching through the trees and bushes and dead logs of the nearby forest the young king noticed a clump of flowers. When he went closer he discovered a pair of smiling eyes staring back at him. An ancient hand reached out,

'Help me up young fella, I'm stuck here.' The king scuttled forward and pulled the old hunter from where he'd gotten stuck.

'Now what is it that you want?' And the king explained. The old hunter gave him a single rosemary then and said.

'When this flower bows in front of a woman, she will be the one that you should marry!'

The young king happily thanked him for the single rosemary. Then he announced throughout his country that every woman who cared to be his queen should attend a party at his court and if his rosemary bows before one of them, then he will marry her.

You can imagine how many pretty women from all over his country came to the king's special party. A crowd formed in the courtyard. The king's majordomo made them take a nice line and the young king came to see them holding the single rosemary in his hand. He stopped in front of every girl but the flower did not bow in front of any of them.

Still, the next day he announced for second time but also in many other countries that he welcomes every sincere and noble woman who wished to be his queen. And this time even more charming ladies came but the rosemary did not bow in front of any of them. And the king tried a third time too, welcoming every girl from all over the world and their origin did not matter. There were many beautiful and lovely girls among them but the rosemary remained as straight as a flagpole. The poor king did not know what to do, he couldn't sleep and his subjects were angry with him as he could not choose one among the many beautiful girls.

One evening the king was lying in his bed, mulling over his problem when a small bird flew into his room. He had golden legs and golden wings and began to speak to the single rosemary.

'Listen, rosemary. I know that the king has much sorrow and I want to help him. Twice he freed me from the claws of a hawk and now he deserves my help.' The golden legged and golden winged bird flew over to the king and perched on his shoulder. 'The girl that rosemary would bow before lives in the fairies' garden. Tomorrow morning you should depart from your court. I will lead you to the fairies' garden.'

The king listened to the bird's talk and could hardly wait until dawn. He rose early and, together, he and the rosemary departed. The bird with golden legs and golden wings flew above them. She led them through the forests, meadows and hills of many countries. During their voyage they arrived at a huge forest where they found a horse lying on his side groaning painfully. The king approached him and the horse begged him,

'Your Majesty, please help me and I will be in your debt. Over a year ago an old witch shot a silver arrow into my side and still nobody has helped me pull it out.'

The king tenderly loosened the arrow and that moment the horse jumped to his feet and turned into a magnificent magic steed.

'Thank you for you kindness, Your Majesty.' The magic steed said. 'I know your heart's desire. Get on my back and I will do my best to help you to find your bride.'

The king jumped onto his back and the horse flew through the clouds as fast as the wind. The single rosemary flew in front of them and the bird with golden legs and golden wings flew above them. But suddenly the magic steed stopped. The king looked around and what do you think he saw? There, far below them, glittering in the sun was a glorious glass castle with glass walls, glass doors, a glass roof and glass windows. And from inside the castle someone was screaming from the top of his lungs. The young king ran into the castle and can you imagine who he saw? Sitting there was another king made of glass gasping as if he were in pain.

'Why are you moaning, glass-king?' the young king asked.

'Why shouldn't I?' The glass-king retorted. 'Can't you see that there is an enormous bumble-bee in my stomach biting me!'

'Well...can I help you to get rid of her?'

'No, unfortunately you can't' the glass-king said. Nobody can do anything while the bumble-bee's mother, the old spider-witch with two swords is still alive.

I used to have a magic steed, he could have killed her but this devilish spider shot my poor horse.'

The glass-king had hardly finished moaning when the spider with the two swords lowered herself from the attic and sat down on the glass sofa beside the queen. Oh! I almost forgot to tell you that the queen, who is also made of glass sat on the glass sofa as well. She was wearing a dress made of roses but she was covered in spider's webs from head to foot. The spider with two swords spun her web around the queen. And when she had finished, a thornbird flew right at the queen and tore the webs off her. No sooner had the thornbird finished tearing away the web than the spider with two swords appeared again and began spinning!

'I can't watch this,' shouted the young king pulling out his sword and striking a blow at the spider. But the wicked spider had two swords so she had a great advantage. As they dueled the young king realized that he couldn't win. And at that moment the spider knocked the sword from his hand and it struck the wall of the glass castle, shattering it. The magic steed heard the noise from the courtyard, galloped at full speed into the throne-room and kicked the spider with his huge hooves. She died immediately on the spot! When the bumble-bee saw that her mother was in a danger, she suddenly zipped out of the glass-king's mouth and the magic steed stepped on to her! It was tremendously exciting for everyone watching!

As soon as the spider and the bumble-bee perished what do you think happened? Wonder of wonders! Everything changed! The glass-king turned into a real king, the glass-queen changed from glass into flesh – oh, what a beautiful queen she was as roses burst into bloom on her dress. The little thornbird changed back into the queen's personal maid. And the glass castle turned into a golden palace.

After all of these fortunate changes, the former glass-king explained to the young king what had caused such unhappiness in his kingdom. An old witch wanted him to marry her daughter. But because he had already found his beautiful bride, the old witch became very angry with him. She turned her own daughter into a bumble-bee and turned him into a glass-king. And she sent her daughter into the glass-king's stomach to torture him. The witch herself changed into a spider with two swords to spin her web around the queen. She also shot the king's magic horse with an arrow.

When the king finished their story he asked the young king.
'How can I help you after you did so much for me?'
'Tell me where I can find the fairies' garden.'
'It is not far from here... my magic steed will take you there.'

The young king did not even stay for supper. He jumped on the magic steed's back and by sunset they were flying through the fragrant air above the fairies' garden.

However, when they descended they found great sorrow there. The fairies were mourning and their diamond palace was covered in black veils.

'Who are you mourning for?' the young king asked them.

'Our princess.' they answered. She turned into a white lily when she heard that a spider with two swords was spinning a web around her sister hour by hour.'

'Please let me visit your white lily.' the king said to the fairies.

They went to the garden and as soon as they reached the lily, the single rosemary bowed in front of her. The bird with golden wings and legs flew to the lily and started to sing. And wonder of wonders! At that moment the white lily trembled and then became a beautiful young woman as dazzling as the sun! The young king shouted in joy.

'You are the one I have been seeking! You are mine and I am yours till death do us part!'

And the princess laughed as they kissed each other. Swiftly they jumped into the carriage and drove to the young king's palace. Well, a splendid wedding was held that very day with great happiness and they both lived happily ever after and for many years to come.

The Princess of the Wind

Once upon a time a very long time ago there lived a king and a queen and their son John. One day while this royal family was enjoying a pleasant afternoon in the castle gardens the king took a sip of his wine, leaned forward in his lounge chair and said,

'My son, you really should have a look around this world. If you want to go away, you have my blessings.'

'And mine too.' the queen added.

Well this was utterly unexpected. Prince John was excited to leave his parent's court and he felt as though he would burst as he said good-bye to his mother and father who's faces looked both happy and sad.

At the beginning of Prince John's voyage he met an extremely tall and thin man. Astonished, because he had never seen anyone like him before, Prince John asked,

'Who are you and what is your profession?'

And the very tall and very thin man said,

'My name is Lightning because I can move faster than a lightning bolt.'

'Really?! I would love to see that,' the prince said excitedly.

He had barely formed these words when a deer jumped out from behind a nearby bush. Lightning leapt forward and in two strides he had caught the deer between his hands. Prince John said,

'I believe you now. You definitely deserve the name 'Lightning'. Would you consider accompanying me on my journcy?'

The tall thin man looked at Price John and smiled widely. They shook hands and then continued down the road together. As they walked along, they came across a man with gigantic shoulders who was lying under a huge mountain.

As they approached the enormous figure the prince asked,

'Who are you and what are you doing?'

And the man with gigantic shoulders said, 'My mother named me 'Mountain-Mover' because I can lift mountains onto my shoulders.'

And sure enough, he picked up that mountain and heaved it onto his shoulders as if it were a sack of wheat!

'Oh, please would you like to come along with us, my friend?' the prince asked.

'With pleasure.' Mountain-Mover' replied. And the prince shook hands with him too and the three of them continued on together.

The trio soon arrived at a thick forest where they met a man whose cheeks were as big and round as bouncing balls. The prince asked him,

'Who are you and what is your profession?'

And the big-cheeked man said, 'My name is 'Blower' and when I blow trees snap to pieces and even the sturdiest houses collapse.'

'You should definitely join our company then.' The prince said. And they all shook hands heartily and continued on their journey together, laughing and joking. The prince was very happy. He felt that he had met the most interesting people in the world!

Soon they came upon a man with an arrow in his hand. The prince greeted him and asked, 'Who are you and what is your profession?'

'People call me 'Archer' as I can hit a pea from the palm of a man's hand with amazing accuracy.'

'Oh, I would love to see your skill for myself,' the prince said delightedly. 'Archer' had a pea tucked away for situations such as this and he gave it to the prince who placed it upon his palm. Everyone watched as 'Archer' walked down the path until he was himself the size of a pea on the horizon. The prince squeezed his eyes shut as 'Archer' let out a mighty yell and pulled back the arrow until the bow was stretched to its limit. Half a moment later the pea disappeared from Prince John's hand and everyone felt confused as 'Archer' came bounding back towards them. 'So?' He said smilingly, 'Impressive isn't it?' Well, 'Archer' hit the pea so accurately that the arrow did not even brush the prince's palm! The prince shook hands with him and they all travelled together down the road.

They did not get very far yet when they met a short man who had enormous ears. The prince greeted him too and asked him,

'Who are you and what is your profession?'

And the short man said,

'My name is 'Listener'. If I put one of my ears on the ground I can listen to anybody's talk even if he is far away from me.'

Listener's answer made the prince laugh and so he asked him to join their company. And they all travelled together until they arrived at the country of the Fairies. The daughter of the fairies' king could run as fast as the wind and she was magically beautiful. Everybody called her 'Princess of the Wind'. The princess wished to marry a fine prince and so her father announced to his kingdom that he would give his daughter to the young man who could out-run her in a race. 'But all who lost would lose their heads!' The king announced, just to make it more exciting.

Of course when Prince John and his companions heard about the competition they all looked at 'Lightning'. They hurried to the royal courtyard, pushed their way to the front of the crowd and Prince John said to the king,

'Your Majesty, my friend would like to try his luck.'

'Very well,' the king replied, 'Ninety-nine young men have lost their heads. Be assured that his head will be the 100th.'

A huge crowd gathered to see whether their beloved princess would beat the very tall and very thin man. The princess started to run but 'Lightning' leapt forward and easily out-ran her. The princess burst into tears in her shame.

The King announced,

'It is true that this man was faster this time but perhaps my daughter did not feel well. Let us hold another race tomorrow.' Murmurs of approval could be heard from the crowd.

That evening, after the sun had gone down and only moon-shadows distorted the land, Prince John crept onto the castle grounds. He remained hidden in some bushes outside of the princess' bedroom window waiting. And then she appeared in all of her loveliness. Oh, how lovely she was! The prince thought.

In the next morning the crowd re-gathered, hooting and jeering and terribly excited. And 'Lightning' out-ran the princess for a second time. She was so ashamed that she ran as fast as she could down into the orchard that adjoined the king's courtyards, far away from everyone.

And the king made an announcement,

'Now, my son,' he said to 'Lightning', 'You've run a better race than my daughter again. But I want you to try your luck a third time as well.' And Lightning agreed.

In the meantime the princess sent a beautiful diamond ring to 'Lightning' as a present. Unfortunately the princess' shame had turned into deviousness, for this was not an ordinary diamond ring, but a magical one. Anyone who placed it on his or her finger would become paralyzed. Of course 'Lightning' had no idea, but someone else did....'Listener'! 'Listener' told 'Archer' to aim for the ring before 'Lightning' started the race.

On the third day, just before the race, the princess and 'Lightning' stood side-by-side. As the shot sounded for it to begin the princess took off very fast but 'Lightning' could not. He stood there as if his feet were paralyzed. At that second 'Archer' swiftly hit the head of the ring, it broke in pieces and fell off the Lightning's finger. He jumped forward and in moments he had out-run the princess for the third time as well.

The princess cried and cried for she did not like the tall and thin man and now she was stuck with him. It was really Prince John who she liked and wished to marry. You can imagine how happy she was when 'Lightning' went to her father the next day and told him that he would prefer to exchange his daughter's hand in marriage for as much gold as his friend could carry on his shoulders.

'You can have them if you can carry them.' the king said happily.

'Mountain-Mover' immediately picked up six carts of gold as if they were nothing for him. Then the king asked his servants to bring another six carts of gold but 'Mountain-Mover' laughed at their grunting and straining and took all of them himself as they watched in astonishment. The king then ordered his servants to collect all of the gold and silver dishes and cutlery in his palace. When it was all collected,' Mountain-Mover' said, 'Now that's enough.' And he and his friends left the king's court with the treasures. But as soon as they had left, the king began scheming over how he could get his wealth back. He decided that he would send the princess after them as if they had kidnapped her! And then he would send his army to rescue her along with his gold. It seemed to be a brilliant idea to the king.

The princess caught up with Prince John and his company quickly and when she arrived Prince John was the happiest man among them all! A short while longer, 'Listener' put one of his ears down to the ground and told his friends,

'Our fate is not good, my friends. The king has sent his army after us. They plan on killing us and taking the princess and the gold back with them to their king.'

'Ah, don't worry about them.' Said 'Blower' with a chortle. 'I will take care of them.' Well, the army arrived at noon. As soon as they got too close, 'Blower' turned back and blew towards them. A tornado sprang up from his mouth, which blew the soldiers with their horses beyond the end of the world.

And the friends with the princess went home in peace to Prince John's father's kingdom. The king and the queen were overjoyed when they saw their son again and were very pleased when they found out that he also brought with him a beautiful princess! In Prince John's palace the friends shared the lot of treasures among them and the prince only asked for the princess' hand. She happily said 'yes' and they had a wonderful wedding the very day. And they still live happily even to this day.

Aloysius

Once upon a time there lived once an old king who was so unfortunate that in his kingdom he did not have the sun, the moon and the stars on the sky. He and his subjects lived in a total darkness and they were always sad. The king used to have three daughters but three dragons kidnapped them. One day he announced in his country that the person who would bring the sun, the moon, the stars and his three daughters back, could marry one of his daughters and could have his kingdom.

A poor widow listened to this announcement and she went to the king and told him,

'I have three brave sons, Your Majesty. Give them horses, swords and money and they bring back to you your daughters, the sun, the moon and the stars.'

'Very well, poor woman,' the king said, 'send your sons to me.'

And it happened like that. But before the three young men appeared in front of the king the youngest man's sister advised him not to choose any of the golden haired horses in the king's stable but only ask for the lame filly from the pit.

The three young men arrived at the king's court and the king gave them enough money and swords and rifles. They went to the stable and the two older brothers chose two beautiful steeds but their youngest brother did not choose any of them. He said he wanted only the lame filly from the pit.

He did not even pick up a heavy and a fancy sword like his older brothers did. He listened to his sister's advice and picked up only a thin and a very flexible sword, which was willing to cut even a piece of stone into two pieces.

The two older brothers rode ahead at full speed on their beautiful steeds and their youngest brother led the lame filly from the city. When they reached the border of the city the filly shook himself, turned into a golden haired steed and he said,

'Come on, little master, get on my back! And tell me, do you wish to go as fast as the wind, or as fast as a flash of lightning, or as swift as a passing thought?

'Either way,' answered the young man, 'as long as neither of us is harmed!'

'I take you directly to the blacksmith of the sky now.' The steed said. 'You have to ask him to have a hundred pounds ball in his fire for you.'

And the steed jumped in the air and in two shakes of a lamb's tail, they were flying through it. The young man closed his eyes for a second as he felt dizzy and when he opened them again they already arrived at the blacksmith of the sky.

The young man greeted him politely and the blacksmith asked him,

'What are you up to, my son?'

And the young man said,

'I would like to ask you a favour. Please put a hundred pounds iron ball into your fire and leave it there until I come back for it.'

'Very well, my son but what is your name?'

And the young man asked him,

'Why don't you give me a name? I would prefer to do that.'

'It's fine with me,' the blacksmith said, 'your name will be Aloysius from now on.'

And Aloysius said good-bye to the blacksmith, jumped on the back on his horse and they were flying through the air again. Soon the steed landed on a bridge made of brass. His brothers were waiting for Aloysius there and they were very surprised when they saw him on the back of a golden haired steed. There was a beautiful meadow beside the brass-bridge and the brothers let their horses to graze there. They lay down and were agreed that their oldest brother would guard at night.

But he soon fell asleep and only Aloysius stayed awake. He left his brothers behind, went under the bridge and pierced the tip of his sword through the bridge. The seven-headed dragon lived near by in his brass castle, which stood on a brass duck's leg and it went around continuously. Soon himself the seven-headed dragon arrived at the bridge on his horse and his horse's foot caught in the tip of Aloysius' sword.

'What's wrong with you?' The seven-headed dragon shouted to his horse. 'Are you afraid of Aloysius? I know you are under the bridge, Aloysius but if you are brave enough, come out and fight with me!'

Aloysius jumped out from under the bridge, pulled out his sword and with one swift stroke he cut off six heads of the seven-headed dragon. At that moment when he cut them off, two ravens were flying over their heads holding some water in their beaks. When the dragon saw them, he called them out,

'Throw a drop of water on me and I give you two dead bodies.'

Aloysius said too,

'You rather throw a drop of water on me and I give you seven dead bodies.' The ravens thought seven bodies were better than two and they threw a drop of water on Aloysius. He immediately felt refreshed and cut off the seventh head of the dragon too.

And he went back to his brothers, lay down beside them and slept until the next morning. They travelled further together and by the evening they arrived at a silver bridge. The twelve-headed dragon lived near by in his silver castle, which stood on a silver turkey's leg and went around continuously. It was their middle brother's turn now to stay awake and be on guard at night. But he fell asleep and only Aloysius was awake again. He went to the silver bridge and pierced the tip of his sword through the bridge.

Soon the twelve-headed dragon arrived on his horse at the bridge and his horse's foot caught in the tip of Aloysius' sword.

'What's wrong with you?' The twelve-headed dragon shouted to his horse. 'Are you afraid of Aloysius? I know you are under the bridge, Aloysius but if you are brave enough come out and fight with me!'

And Aloysius jumped out from under the bridge, pulled out his sword and with one swift stroke he cut off eleven heads of the twelve-headed dragon. At that moment when he cut them off, two ravens were flying over their heads holding some water in their beaks. When the dragon saw them, he called them out,

'Throw a drop of water on me, I give you two dead bodies and you can live in my silver forest.'

Aloysius said too,

'You rather throw a drop of water on me and I give you twelve dead bodies and you can live in the silver forest.' The ravens thought twelve bodies were better than two and they threw a drop of water on Aloysius. He immediately felt refreshed and cut off the twelfth head of the dragon.

The brothers spent the third night beside the golden bridge and Aloysius killed the twenty-four headed dragon there at the very same way as he did it before with the two other dragons. Finally he told his brothers,

'Let's go and have a look at the dragons' castles! There are three castles not far from here. The first belongs to the seven-headed dragon, the second belongs to the twelve-headed dragon and the third belongs to the twenty-four-headed dragon.'

His older brothers answered,

'We don't' go, we are afraid of the dragons.'

'Don't be afraid, I already killed them while you were sleeping.' Aloysius said. Let's go and find out what their castles hide.'

And they first went to the castle of the seven-headed dragon. It stood on a brass duck's leg and went around fast. Aloysius shouted,

'Stop, revolving castle!'

'You are not my master!' the castle shouted back and Aloysius shouted again,

'I am your new master!' And that moment the castle stopped. The three young men went inside and in one of the rooms of the castle they found the oldest daughter of their king. And what do you think happened next? At that moment when they found the oldest princess, the sun shone in the old king's country!

You can imagine how happy the oldest princess was. And the brothers went to the castle of the twelve-headed dragon. They found there the younger princess. And when they found her the moon rose in the old king's country! The two princesses were overjoyed, they embraced each other and asked the brothers to bring their youngest sister too. And the three young men went to the twenty-four-headed dragon's castle and they found the youngest princess there. She was as beautiful as the dazzling sun. And when the brothers found her, the stars rose in the old king's country!

But the dragons had a sister who was an old witch and had such a big mouth like a huge bathtub. She had two daughters and when she realized that the brothers were on their way with the princesses, she asked her older daughter to precede the travelling group and to turn herself into a pear-tree having a lot of pears. The brothers will see the pear-tree, they will eat of its pears and they will die of them.

The girl obeyed her mother's wish and the three young men who travelled ahead found soon a pear-tree beside the road with full of ripped and tasty pears. The two older brothers were very thirty. They ran to the tree to tear some pears from it but Aloysius stood in front of them and did not let them to do. He pulled out his sword and ran through the pear-tree with it. And what do you think he saw? Blood was flowing from the tree and the old witch's daughter's wailing could be heard from the depths of the earth. She died there.

Now the old witch sent her younger daughter to change herself into a spring. The witch wanted the three young men to drink from the water of the spring and to die of it. So the witch's daughter turned into a spring and when the two older brothers saw it they wanted to drink from its water, as they were very thirsty. But Aloysius did not let them to do that. He knew what kind of spring it was. He stubbed his sword into the spring and blood was flowing from it. So the old witch's younger daughter died too.

Now it was the old witch's turn. She opened her huge mouth and blew such an ice-cold wind towards them that they immediately became half frozen. Aloysius put down the youngest princess then on the ground from his saddle and flew on his steed to the blacksmith of the sky.

'Do you see, dear master that huge mouth on the ground?' he asked the blacksmith.

'I can see it, my son.'

'Now if you see it, throw the hundred pounds, red-hot iron ball into that mouth.'

And the blacksmith of the sky picked up the red-hot iron ball and threw it into the old witch's mouth. And the old witch burned immediately and turned into dust on the spot.

The three young men with the three princesses safely arrived in the old king's palace. The old king was enjoying the sunset in his garden when they appeared in front of him. What do you know? Everybody was overjoyed and the three young men married the three princesses the very day. They had a splendid wedding and the old king gave his whole kingdom to Aloysius. You cannot imagine a happier couple than him and his bride! And this is the end of my tale.

The Poor Man's Kingdom

There lived once a poor man with a kind heart. He and his wife loved entertaining guests in the evenings so much that if they didn't have a friend scheduled to visit then the poor man would go into the street and invite the first passer-by in for some supper and conversation. Their table was modest but their company was delightful.

One evening the king himself was walking on the poor man's street disguised as a pauper. When the kind-hearted man caught sight of him he promptly invited him in for dinner. Of course the poor man did not know who his guest really was, but he and his wife had a wonderful time with the disguised royal, eating and drinking and making each other laugh. And in the middle of all of this fellowship, the kind host suddenly said, 'Oh, I wish I were a king!' and his wife replied 'In your dreams, dear.'

The real king did not say a word, he just smiled and thanked them both for the delicious supper and then made his way into the street. Once he was back at his palace, he called his servants and asked them to bring the poor man, while still asleep, to the palace, and tuck him into his royal bed.

And so the servants brought the sleeping man from his humble home and slipped him between the silk sheets and soft pillows of the king's royal sleeping spot. Well, you can imagine how surprised he was when he woke up in a golden canopy bed the next morning! He was sure that he was dreaming and so he pinched himself...and then pinched himself harder. But it was not a dream. Servants immediately entered his room, bowing and smiling.

'Breakfast, Your Majesty?' asked one.

'Shall we draw you a bath, Your Majesty?' asked another.

'Would you like a book, Your Majesty?' asked yet another.

'What do you wish, Your Majesty?' they asked all together.

The poor man shook his head vigorously, 'No, no! I am not a king, who are you?'

'You certainly are, Your Majesty,' the servants said, ignoring his question.

'If I am really a king...then...bring me my crown!' The poor man said feeling helpless and hopelessly confused. The servants ran out and returned with a golden crown encrusted with precious stones. They held up a mirror and the poor man hesitantly placed the magnificent decoration upon his head. The figure reflected back at him shocked him out of his good sense. He really did look like a king!

So he calmed down and took a bath in the diamond bathtub with a magnificent view of the mountains and sky. The servants then dressed him in gold and velvet clothing. He ate his breakfast with golden cups and plates and golden forks and spoons. Oh, it really was the grandest time he had ever had! Following breakfast the servants accompanied him to the throne room where he held court for the entire day. The real king hid himself behind a curtain to watch him and he enjoyed the situation very much.

However the poor fellow's reign over the kingdom was short-lived. That night when he had fallen asleep the servants carried him above their heads on pillows and delivered him back to his own bed in his humble home. As soon as he opened his eyes in the morning, his wife began quarreling, 'Where were you all day yesterday, didn't even come home last night?' She was washing dishes, but water was splashing all over the poor fellow, his eyes stinging from the soap. 'You left me without saying a word.'

Barely able to open his eyes, he blurted out, 'You cannot talk to me in this manner woman…Look at me, I am the king!'

'Are you mad?!' She looked at him carefully and then they began to quarrel very loudly. The whole village gathered outside their window to listen.

Finally the king also arrived, he was curious about the poor man's behaviour and he came to see how he was doing after his day of royal treatment.

'Why do you quarrel?' the king asked them.

'My husband has gone crazy, Your Majesty,' said the wife, 'he thinks that he is a king!'

'Well, never mind, don't quarrel, both of you come to my palace and live with me.' And so the poor fellow and his wife moved to the king's palace where they lived as barons. However, the two spent more money than the king gave them and they were always begging for more. Finally the king became fed up with them and said, 'You could spend Darius' treasures, my friends. If you come to me for money once more, I will chase you out of my court!' But, unfortunately, the poor fellow's mind was becoming too cunning now that he was living so high and mighty. He thought, 'Wait a minute, my king. I am sure that I can make you open your purse for me.'

He went and asked his wife to go to the queen and tell her that he had died and that she did not have enough money for a proper funeral. So she went to the queen crying and moaning, 'Oh, Majestic Queen, my sweet husband is dead, please help me…' Of course the queen felt so sorry for her and gave her a bag of gold. The cunning husband and wife spent it all in only a few days. Then the poor man went to the king and said that his wife had died and he did not have money to bury her. He cried so much that the king felt sorry for the poor fellow. To ease his mind, the king gave him a bag of gold for the funeral.

Later on, the queen joined her husband in the throne room for an afternoon tea. 'I heard that your poor man has died.' She said.

The king pursed his lips thoughtfully, 'No, you must be mistaken, dear wife. He is quite alive, I saw him only this afternoon. I think you mean that his wife has passed away.'

'No, no, not his wife, I saw her this morning when she asked me for money for her husband's funeral.'

The king and the queen started to quarrel and after quarter of an hour, their quarreling had come to no conclusion so they decided to go to the poor man's apartment to find out the truth.

Lucky for him, the poor man was enjoying the view out of the window and so he saw the king and queen approaching. Quickly he sprung into action. He lit two candles and he and his wife lay down on the floor and covered themselves with a black sheet.

When the king and queen stepped into their room and saw the dead couple, the queen began to cry, 'You see, my dear husband, they are both dead.'

'Really, it does seem that they are dead,' the king replied 'but I would like to know which of them died first. I'd give a sack of gold to the person who could tell me this.'

Hearing this, the poor man jumped to his feet and said, 'I died first, Your Majesty!'

The king had a good laugh at him and then ordered his servants to give a sack of gold to the poor and foolish fellow.

'And now it's time for both of you to go home and live your lives as before.' The king said. And so the poor man and his wife returned to their village but they did not live as they had before. They bought a healthy piece of farmland along with some cows. They tilled the soil and milked the cows and soon they had become the wealthiest couple in the village. Every evening the laughter and happiness of guests filled their warm home. And they lived happily ever after, happier than they would ever have been as a king and a queen.

The Lizard-Face Princess

Once upon a time in a land far, far away there lived a king, a queen and their twelve sons. The twelve princes were adventurous young men and they often spent their days wandering in the never-ending forests that surrounded their parents' palace. One day while frolicking beneath the foliage the princes met an old man who greeted them politely and said,

'Why don't you leave your father's court, Your Highnesses, and go discover the world?' Well, the old man's question rang in their heads as they returned to the palace. That night each prince had miraculous dreams of high adventure and excitement. And in the morning they were ready to embark on a grand journey. So they said good-bye to their father and mother and made their way down the lane and over the hill and into the beyond.

By the evening they had arrived at a beautiful castle. Inside they found twelve bedrooms with beds that were prepared for the night. In the dining room they found a table laden with sumptuous meal and wine. Beside the castle in a hilly meadow nestled a well-built stable for twelve horses. There was a lot of hay and oat for them to feed on. The princes led their horses into the stall where they could feed. They themselves were also very hungry so they went back to the castle, sat down and ate their dinner. After dinner they all went to bed and slept soundly.

At midnight the eldest prince woke up. He heard someone calling him by his name,

'Michael come out. Michael...Michael...'

The prince tiptoed out into the courtyard where he found a girl who had the face of a lizard. And the girl began speaking as soon as he was outside,

'Don't be afraid of me, prince, I am a princess and I have eleven sisters just like you have eleven brothers. A witch has cursed us with lizard faces until the day when twelve princes will have lived in this very castle for seven years, seven months, seven days and seven hours without ever leaving it even once.' The prince listened to her speak with fascination, but before he knew it, the lizard-face princess said no more and disappeared as if the earth had swallowed her up.

The next morning Michael told his brothers everything that had happened including what the princess had said. They laughed heartily, 'Dear brother,' they said, 'even if the girls were angels we still would not stay in this palace for seven years, seven months, seven days and seven hours.' And they mounted their horses and left, leaving Michael all alone. However, as soon as they had galloped out of the palace's courtyard, twelve dragons blocked their way. They were unable to pass the fierce monsters and were forced to turn back.

They were hungry again and the eleven princes searched the castle for food. But they could not find any in all the rooms. Only Michael was able to find some and he gave his brothers a little to eat from what he had. The following morning the younger brothers again prepared themselves to leave the castle. But as soon as they trotted away from the castle they turned into marble statues.

So Prince Michael was left alone in the quiet castle that was now guarded by the gallant statues of his brothers. He could not see or hear a living soul anywhere in the castle but both he and his horse always had more than enough to eat and drink. Years and years had passed. After seven years, seven months and four days, the lizard-face princess visited Michael in the evening,

'Listen carefully to me prince. Tonight you'll be visited by eleven devils and they will look just like your brothers. They'll ask you to go with them but you must not listen to them even when they become angry and try to hurt you. Please do this all for me.'

And so at midnight the devils arrived just as the princess said, disguised as his brothers and they called from outside his window,

'Come with us Michael, come with us, we are finally free!! Leave this castle and you'll be safe too, you'll see!'

When the prince did not speak, the devils became angry and beat him. Still he did not follow them. In the morning the lizard-face princess came to Michael's room and spread a magical lotion over his body. And the prince became seven times more handsome and seven times healthier than before!

'You were successful with the first trial, prince,' said the princess, 'but the next trial tonight will be even more difficult. The devils will come again and this time they will look like your mother and father. Again, they will ask you to leave this place but don't say a word. When they realize that they're being ignored they will tie your hands and legs and drag you to the courtyard where they'll hang you by your ankles. Only think of me and don't be afraid of anything in the world!'

Everything happened exactly as the lizard-face princess had said. The devils came disguised as Michael's parents and they beckoned him to leave the castle with them. But he did not say a word. They became so angry that they tied his hands and legs and hung him in the courtyard by his ankles. But in the morning the lizard-face princess came again, cut the rope and spread a magical lotion all over the prince's body. And the prince became healthier and more handsome than before. And at that moment the lizard-face princess lost her lizard features on her right side and half of her beautiful face was revealed!

'Listen carefully, Michael,' she said. 'If you pass the third and final trial, my face and my sisters' faces will return to our normal human forms again. Tonight the devils will come once more, this time disguised as your friends. If you won't agree to go with them they will torture you but just think of me please, resist and do not be afraid.'

And everything happened just as the lizard-face princess had predicted. At midnight the devils arrived asking the prince to come with them.

'Don't waste your life for this lizard girl,' they snarled.

And when he did not listen to them, they tortured him. The next morning the princess arrived and once again spread the magical lotion all over the prince's body. And then he became seven times more handsome. 'Now prince Michael,' the princess said, 'look at my face. I am no longer lizard-face, am I?'

'No, you're not,' the prince answered, 'actually, you look the loveliest and the most beautiful girl I have ever seen,' and he blushed a little.

'Thank you Michael, now go ahead to my city and I'll stay here with my sisters. Later we will follow you. During your voyage you will meet a beautiful girl who will ask you to go with her but you mustn't say a word to her. Later on your journey you will come across a table covered with delicious food and drinks but don't touch anything!'

The prince vowed to do as she said. They bid each other good-bye and Prince Michael mounted his horse and travelled towards the princess' city. When he finally reached the border, a very beautiful girl made him stop,

'Who are you my handsome man? Come with me!' She smiled at him but the prince turned away and continued along his way. He had not gone very far when he saw a table full of delicious food and drinks. Well, his stomach was knotted from hunger and so he thought 'It cannot be such a big deal if I eat only a small piece of bread and drink a small flask of wine.' Well, as soon as the bread and wine hit his stomach he fell from his horse and fell fast asleep on the ground.

And the princess arrived soon after in a gold and velvet carriage to the spot where Prince Michael was sleeping. She tried to awaken him but she couldn't. So she took her golden pen and wrote a message on the prince's sword:

'Dear Prince,

When you wake up, please return to the castle. You will find a nail in the stable's window. Use your sword to cut it in two and your eleven brothers will come back to life. Bring them all to my city. During your voyage you'll reach the shores of the Red Sea. You'll find a giant there who will carry you across the water but when you reach the other side, tell the giant that your ring fell into the sea and ask him to go back and fetch it. As soon as he turns his back, push him into the water. If you don't do this he'll kill you and your brothers. Not far from the Red Sea there are three glass mountains that serve as the gateway to my city. Your horses cannot go through them, but you'll find a goblin living there. He'll try to talk to you but you mustn't answer him. He'll then become very angry and he'll pick you all up and throw you across the Glass Mountains. And you'll fall down right in the centre of my city!'

It was already dark when Prince Michael woke up and read the message. He thought that the princess was really very wise! He immediately mounted his horse and rode back to the palace, ran to the stable and found the nail in one of the windows. With his sword he cut it into two and at that moment the whole castle sounded with joy as his eleven brothers came back to life!

They couldn't believe that they had slept for over seven years! Happily they all feasted in celebration of their return. After the feast all twelve princes mounted their horses and rode in the direction of the princess' city. They travelled seven days and seven nights until they reached the shores of the Red Sea. As the princess predicted, the giant at the shore picked up the twelve princes and their twelve horses and carried them across the water. When they had reached the other side, Prince Michael remembered the princess' note. He told the giant that his favourite ring had fallen into the sea during the journey and would he mind going back to look for it?

As soon as the giant turned his back, Prince Michael pushed him with all his might and with a huge splash he fell into the sea. Sinking and sputtering the giant shouted,

'You were smart enough, human rascal, pushing me into the sea. Otherwise I would have killed all of you!'

'I wasn't smart but my princess was,' Michael thought. And the twelve princes got on their horses and rode away as fast as the wind. By noon they arrived at the foot of the three Glass Mountains. The goblin that lived there caught sight of them and immediately began to babble.

'Who are you and what are you looking for? This is my land and you cannot go any further. I say, tell me who you are, and what you're doing here. I am the owner of these mountains and no one gets past me without a chat.'

The twelve princes laughed at this funny creature but they did not say a word. The goblin became very angry with them and he picked up the horses and the princes and threw them one by one across the Glass Mountains.

And they all fell into a huge straw-stack in the middle of the city. Locals led the princes to the palace where the twelve beautiful princesses were waiting for them in the courtyard. And so twelve dazzling faces met the princes. Well, they had a splendid celebration and every prince and every princess married the very next day and they lived happily ever after.

Mike and His Goat

There once lived a handsome and adventurous young man named Mike who owned two things: a stick, and a goat. He had many problems with his goat. It was very stubborn and rarely obeyed him. Well, one day Mike lost his temper and threw his stick at the goat and, strangely, the stick disappeared. He ran in the direction of the space where his stick vanished and found a big hole in the ground.

The hole was about his size and, without thinking he jumped into it and fell for a long time. He continued to fall for seven days and seven nights when he finally reached a magical place that, he soon learned, was called Fairyland. Mike looked around and his eyes took in everything. There were lush meadows with rippling golden grasses and rivers full of glistening fish and golden birds rustling and singing in the trees. And then suddenly he spotted, between the gently waving trees, a shining palace looking magnificent.

As he made his way towards the palace, he listened as the birds sang glorious songs about the fairies' king. When he arrived at the palace the doors opened for him and inside he found a magnificent feast. In the ballroom many people and many creatures were dancing merrily in celebration of the oldest fairy princess' wedding. The king stepped forward and welcomed Mike as their guest. And he danced with the most beautiful and youngest fairy princess all night. In the morning the princess gave him a golden stick.

'This is a magic stick, Mike. Any living thing you touch with it will die. Any object you touch, will shrivel up so small that you can put it in your pocket.'

Mike thanked the princess for the present and left the festivities. He travelled for one day until he reached a brass castle. A beautiful girl leant out of one of the castle's windows.

'Good day maiden.'

'Good day to you, young man.'

'What are you doing in this castle?'

'I am a princess with an unhappy fate. The seven-headed dragon has kidnapped me from my father's palace. If you would be so kind to rescue me...'

The princess didn't even finish her sentence as the doors of the brass castle flew open from the impact of the seven-headed dragon's club. Oh, he was ferocious and terribly scary as he breathed flames from all of his seven heads. When he saw Mike he became very angry but Mike was not afraid of him. He pulled out his golden stick and struck a blow at the dragon. And right before their eyes, the seven-headed dragon fell to the ground. He was dead.

Well, imagine that you are a princess that has been trapped by such a beast for as long as this princess! You too would be overwhelmed by your freedom! The princess was very happy indeed and she thanked for her rescue to Mike.

Before they departed Mike touched the brass castle with his golden stick and it turned into a brass apple, which he put in his pocket. And Mike and the princess travelled together.

They soon came across another palace. It was made of silver and another princess was leaning out of one of its window. A fourteen-headed dragon had kidnapped her. The princess warned Mike to run away as quickly as he could. However, when the fourteen-headed dragon appeared with his nostrils aflame and his tail swinging to and fro, Mike simply touched him with his golden stick and he immediately slipped away into the clutches of death. The princess of the silver castle screeched in joy and ran down the stairs of the castle to meet Mike and the princess of the brass castle. Mike touched the silver castle with his golden stick and it turned into a silver apple, which he also put in his pocket.

Now Mike and the two princesses were on their way together. Soon they arrived at a golden castle where another lovely princess was leaning out of the window. Mike called to her,

'We want to leave this underworld behind and return to the surface. Would you like to come with us?'

'I wish I could come,' she said as she heaved a deep sigh, 'but the twenty four headed dragon that kidnapped me from my father's palace would kill me if I were to leave.'

'Don't be frightened.' Mike said, 'I will look after the twenty-four headed dragon. I've already killed two other dragons and he'll be the third one.'

He could hardly finish his sentence when a thunderous sound came from the depths of the golden forest, which was around the palace. And then...SMASH, the twenty-four headed dragon's club slammed into the palace's door and he broke through breathing hot flames from every nostril in his twenty-four heads. Mike became so frightened when he saw him that he nearly turned around and ran as fast as he could.

The dragon saw Mike and said, 'What are you looking for in my castle, you rascal?'

'I'm looking for fulfill your fate.' He said and used his golden stick to strike a blow against the dragon that fell on the ground in agony until death took over him.

This princess immediately jumped into Mike's arms and kissed him squarely on his cheek. 'Now,' she said, 'let's go to the surface, I'm really tired of the underworld.' Then Mike touched the golden castle with his golden stick and it turned into a golden apple. He slipped it into his pocket.

They travelled for many days. During the nights, they nestled together in leaves and pine needles. Finally they reached the bottom of the hole where Mike had fallen into the underworld. Well, they all wanted to return to the surface, but none of them knew how. Their situation seemed quite desperate when suddenly Mike heard the bleating of his goat.

'I think that's my goat,' he said as a joyous smile slowly spread across his lips. 'Is that you, dear goat?' And the goat recognized his master's voice immediately and he happily bleated again.

'Run to the village please,' Mike asked him, 'and collect all the rope that you can find. Tie them together and let one end down to us so that me and the three princesses can climb out.'

'Will you ever beat me again?' the goat asked.

'No, never. Just run now, run. And bring lots of rope from the village.' And so the goat trotted as fast as his legs would take him. He found lots of rope in the village, tied them to his tail and let them down into the hole.

While the goat was in the village, the princesses flattered Mike and asked for the three apples. They were cheeky enough to ask for the golden stick too. And Mike gave away all of these things to them. After that they were agreed that the princess from the brass castle would climb out first to the surface, then the princess from the silver castle and finally the princess from the golden castle will follow them. And Mike will be the last one to be freed from the underworld.

The goat was very helpful as he gently pulled each princess to the surface, one after the other. However, when all three princesses were safely above ground, they decided to allow the goat to pull Mike only halfway up but then they were going to cut the rope! He was not a prince and they did not want to waste their time with him anymore. But Mike was not as foolish as they thought. He wanted to know whether he could trust the princesses or they were planning to trick him. So he tied a big rock to the rope and his goat began pulling. And sure enough, the wily princesses cut the rope with a sharp stone. And the rock fell down and almost hit Mike.

Well, Mike was disappointed in the princesses and he shouted for his goat for help from the bottom of the hole, but the girls had taken him away. He could do nothing and so, decided wasting no time, he returned to the fairies' palace. The youngest fairy princess recognized him right away. 'It's so nice to see you, Mike. Did my golden stick help you? Why have you come back?'

The poor lad sadly explained what had happened.

'Don't worry Mike. This time I'll give you a diamond stick. It can do everything that your golden stick did before, but it has an extra benefit. If you touch the three princesses' palaces with it, they will turn into a diamond apple and if you touch the apple, it will turn into one diamond palace.'

'Thank you for your present, fairy princess, but what can I do with a diamond stick if I cannot go back to the surface?'

The princess smiled warmly, 'Just listen to your good heart, Mike and you'll find your way back.'

Mike said good-bye to the fairy princess and was on his way again. He travelled day and night and finally arrived at a tree that was so tall that its highest branch reached the top of the sky. On that branch rested an eagle's nest with six babies inside. Mike then spotted a gigantic snake coiled around the tree's trunk, slowly making its way up towards the nest.

'I can't let that snake devour those babies,' he thought to himself. He caught hold of one of the tree's lower branches and climbed up, so that he was within reach of the snake. When he was close enough, he pulled out his diamond stick and struck a blow against its gigantic coiled body. And then it fell, struck dead.

The little eaglets were so happy, they began flapping and dancing around their nest. They told Mike that their mother would be very grateful when she heard how heroically they had been saved, when all at once a big black cloud appeared above their nest. It was their mother who had returned with lots of food under her wings. She was not happy to see Mike at all,

'Mark my words, you human rascal, this is your last hour.'

But the baby eaglets then described in dramatic details what happened and they begged their mother not to harm Mike.

'It was a gigantic snake, mama,' said one.

'He wanted eat us, mama. We were really scared.'

'Okay, shush' said their mother. 'That's enough.' And she turned to Mike. 'Is this true? How can I show you my gratitude for saving my youngsters?'

'Oh,' said Mike, heaving a deep sigh, 'I would like to return to the surface, but I don't know how.'

'This is not a problem,' said the eagle, 'I will take you there. Just give me a few moments.' And she filled a satchel with food and threw it around her neck. Then she asked Mike to sit on her back and she took off. Soon she asked Mike to give her a piece of meat from the satchel. In fact she asked him for some meat regularly along the way. And soon the satchel became empty.

'Give me some more meat,' the eagle suddenly said, 'or I cannot fly any further.'

Mike panicked because there was no more meat. In his despair he took out his pocketknife, cut a piece of his own thigh and threw it to the eagle.

'I can tell that the last piece you gave me was a piece of human flesh,' she said. 'It has made me so strong that I can take you to the surface now.' And soon they reached the top of the hole, where the eagle let Mike off onto the ground. Mike said thank you and the eagle flew back to her eaglets.

And Mike was on his way again. He had to find his goat, he thought. Soon enough, he suddenly heard bleating coming from a distance. He made his way in that direction. Well, suddenly he caught sight of three castles: the brass castle, the silver castle and the golden castle all standing beside each other. The bleating of Mike's goat was getting louder and finally he could see that his goat was standing in front of the door of the golden castle.

'Oh, dear goat, how wonderful to see you!' Mike shouted. 'Where are the princesses?'

'They all went home to their father's kingdom and got married. And they left me behind to guard the three castles. It's so boring though.'

'Watch this.' And Mike touched the three castles with his diamond stick and they turned into a diamond apple. And then he touched the diamond apple with his stick and it turned into the most majestic palace anyone had ever seen. However, when he walked inside and admired the rooms, he could not feel happy.

'How lucky the princesses are to have found their mates. I wish I have found mine!' he thought. 'I wish the youngest fairy princess were here!'

Before he had finished this sentence, his goat jumped before him and sitting on his back, there she was, the youngest, loveliest and the most beautiful daughter of the fairies' king! And they flung their arms around each other.

Well, a splendid wedding was held that very day. The fairies' king whole court attended and the eagle and her eaglets were special guests. There was great happiness and merrymaking. Mike and the fairy princess lived happily for many years to come. And that is the end of my tale. Put it on the frozen river, and let it slide hither and thither.

The Three Golden Rings

Once upon a time, many years ago, there lived a widowed king and his handsome son. The royal advisers believed that the young prince should have a mother so they encouraged the king to marry again. Then one day, this is just what the king did. He married the Burkus Queen who happened to be a widow herself and she also had a son. For this reason the king thought she would make a suitable match. Well, we shall see just how suitable she was.

While the queen ensured that her son dressed in velvet outfits trimmed with gold, she gave the king's son only the most bedraggled old clothes. The poor soul looked like a beggar and the king did not like his appearance at all. He asked the queen why his son always looked dirty and unkempt while the queen's son looked so very sophisticated. And she replied,

'You see, my dear husband, this is the true nature of your son. I have dressed him to look like a proper prince and he then rolls around in the dirt to make himself look like a pauper. Frankly, I don't think he appreciates nice things. Believe me, I've tried.'

The queen always spoke about the prince so negatively that the king's heart grew cold towards him. And then, one day, the king said, 'If this is the true nature of my son then I don't want to raise him as my heir, the future king. He'll have to go to the meadow and look after my golden-haired flock of sheep as a shepherd.'

And so the prince was sent away. Sadly, he left, but he did not go to the meadow. He had no interest in being a shepherd. Instead he wandered without any direction and by nightfall he had arrived at a thick forest. He heaved a deep sigh and said to himself,

'I cannot lie down here because of the beast that lives in the shadows of this wood.' As soon as he said this, someone began to speak somewhere above his head.

'Don't be afraid, dear prince, you won't be hurt, just climb up this tree.' The prince looked up the tree and saw a little house among its branches. He did not think too much but climbed up the tree and into the little house. Who do you think he found? Well, an old man with a white beard that fell to his knees was sitting beside a table with a book in his lap.

The prince said 'hello' and the old man placed the book before him,

'Read, my son,' it was all he said.

And so the prince began to read and as he read he forgot his hunger and his sadness. When he had finished he fell asleep and didn't wake until the next morning when the old man whispered, 'I know who you are my son, I also know your sad story. Listen to me and you won't regret it.' The eyes of the young prince fluttered open to find the kindly ancient eyes of the old man peering back at him. The old man stroked his beard thoughtfully and then began speaking again, his gaze turning away from his sleepy young guest.

'Go to the Black King's country and offer yourself as a goose boy. The Black King will ask you to look after his flock of one hundred geese. As soon as you drive these geese to a meadow, they'll fly in a hundred different directions. No goose boy has ever been able to keep them together. I'll give you a magic whistle and when the geese hear it, they'll flock to you immediately.' The old man got up and pulled a finely crafted wooden whistle from a drawer in his writing table.

'When you have served a year he will ask you what you wish. Only choose his lame filly, don't choose anything else.' And the old man turned back to his book and began to read. He seemed to have forgotten all about the prince.

The prince slapped his hands against his thighs and pulled himself to his feet as he thanked the old man for his good advice. He was about to leave when the old man suddenly stopped him,

'Wait a second, my son.'

The prince raised his eyebrows,

'Take these three golden rings. On the first evening when you take the geese home, tie the smallest ring to the end of your whip. The Black King's only daughter, who is very lovely, will see it and ask you for it. But you mustn't give it to her unless she shows you what is hidden behind her left ear. On the following day, tie the middle ring to the end of your whip, but when the princess asks to see it, ask her to show you what is hidden behind her right ear. On the third day, tie the largest ring to the end of your whip. Of course the princess will ask you for it, but first she must show you what she has hidden on her forehead.'

The prince thanked the old man for the rings and then made his way in the direction of the Black King's City. When he arrived at the city he went straight to the king and offered his services.

'You've come at the right time,' chortled the king, 'it seems that I need a goose boy. If you serve me for one year which means three days here, and you don't lose any of my precious geese then I won't cut your head off and, best of all, I'll fulfill any of your wishes.'

The following morning the geese were flapping and honking along behind him and he noticed that they began to fly in a hundred different directions. He thought to himself, you can fly wherever you want, I know that you'll come back by the evening.' And he lay down under a tree and slept for the rest of the day. By the evening he got up and blew his whistle hard. And the one hundred geese flew towards him from every direction. The prince tied his smallest ring to the end of his whip and cracked it hard as he marched the geese back to the king's courtyard.

The princess was leaning out of one of the palace windows and she watched as the prince returned with his flock. The shining golden ring on the end of the lad's whip suddenly dazzled her. Oh, she was amazed! She thought that she was just seeing things. After all, how was it possible that a poor goose boy had such a beautiful golden ring?

'I will see for myself,' she thought.

Well, the king was very surprised when he counted the geese and found none of them missing. 'Brilliant job, boy' was all he said before going back to his palace to lie down for the night. But the princess did not lie down. She silently slipped away from the palace and went to find the goose boy.'

'Listen to me, lad, I saw your beautiful golden ring. Give it to me. You're too poor to own such a ring.'

'With pleasure,' said the prince, 'but first please show me what sign you have behind your left ear.

'I cannot do that,' the princess answered, 'nobody but my father my mother and my old nurse can know about it.'

'Well, then I won't give you the ring.'

The princess longed for the ring so much that suddenly she pulled her hair to the side and the prince peered behind her ear. And what do you think he saw? Glittering there was a star so bright that the prince had to close his eyes for a moment. Without any hesitation he gave the ring to the princess and she happily skipped back to the palace.

The second day passed in a similar way to the first. The prince drove the one hundred geese home in the evening but this time he tied the middle ring to the end of his whip. Of course when everybody had gone to sleep in the palace, the princess ran off to see the goose boy begging him for the ring. The prince only gave it to her when she showed him the sign behind her right ear. And what do you think he saw when she brushed back her beautiful hair? It was a brilliant silver moon that emanated a mysterious light. The prince was dazzled by it.

On the third evening the prince tied the biggest golden ring to the end of his whip which he cracked as he walked along the city's streets. People emerged from their houses to admire the goose boy who was becoming well known for keeping the flock of one hundred geese together. The king anxiously approached the boy about his wish.

'Well, you've been successful, my son, now tell us, what is your wish?'

'You have a lame filly in your court, Your Majesty, I would love to have him.' The king started to laugh, 'You are a fool my son,' he said. 'What would you do with that lame filly? Go to my stable and choose a beautiful steed from among my horses.'

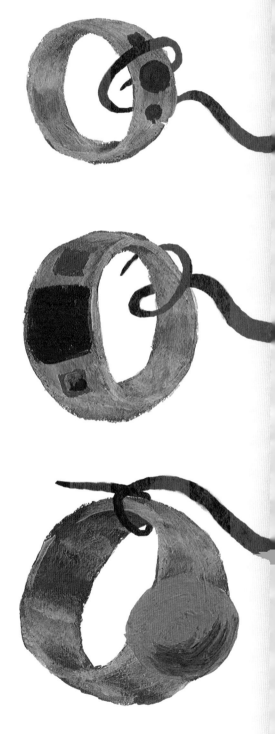

But the prince did not want any beautiful steed. He only wanted the lame filly just as the old man had advised him. The king tried to persuade him, finally he became tired and gave the lame filly to the prince.

As soon as he was gone the princess slipped out from her bedroom again and ran to see the goose boy. She flattered him to give her the third golden ring as well. 'But only,' the prince said, 'if you show me what kind of sign you have on your beautiful forehead.'

What should the princess do? She had already showed him the other two signs and she didn't seem to have any choice. Slowly, she drew back a veil of hair and the prince nearly became blind! A sparkling magnificent sun shone from her forehead. The prince then gave the last ring to the princess and they said good night. The princess returned to the palace and the prince lay down in the hen house.

When he woke up in the morning he searched for an old bridle, which he put on his lame filly's head. Together they walked to the city. But the filly collapsed after two steps.

The prince embraced him around his neck and began to pull him through the city streets. Night had fallen when they reached the border of the forest. The lame filly suddenly shook himself there and turned into a golden-haired six legged magic steed, 'Come on, dear master,' he said, ' get on my back! And tell me, how fast shall we go?'

'As fast as a passing though my sweet horse.'

And the magic steed neighed from the top of his lungs and flew up into the air and in a flash they arrived at the tree where the old man lived. The prince climbed up the tree, knocked on a small door and politely greeted the old man.

'Don't waste any more time here.' The old man said. 'There is a spring not far from here. Go and bathe there. I'll give you a golden towel to dry yourself. Here is a walnut. Inside you'll find a golden outfit covered in diamonds. Put it on and return to the Black King's court where you served so well as a goose boy. The king recently announced that he wanted his daughter to marry the person who could discover the signs behind her ears and on her forehead. Many princes and barons and counts will try their luck. You must wait until all other suitors have had a chance and then make your debut! Doubtless, you will win the princess.'

Well, the prince was grateful for the old man's advice. He jumped on his magic steed's back and they flew off to the spring. After bathing he dried himself with a golden towel and opened the walnut. When he had dressed himself, I can assure you that a more handsome prince could not be found in the whole world! He jumped onto his magic horse's back and galloped off to the king's courtyard.

The palace grounds were packed with noblemen of every sort. Such a huge crowd had gathered that the prince could hardly move. However, as the day went on, the crowd thinned. Finally, the prince stepped forward and politely greeted the king and bowed before the princess. When the princess saw him, she immediately recognized him although she couldn't believe how much the goose boy had changed. Of course she knew that he would win. And then, slowly and surely, the prince recited the signs. A shining star behind her left ear, a glorious moon behind her right ear and a sparkling sun on her beautiful forehead.

'You have guessed right, prince!' exclaimed the amazed king. If my daughter will agree to marry you, then you have my blessings! And I'll give you half of my kingdom, too.'

'Let the festivities begin.' said the princess happily. They wedded that very day and everyone in the country for far around danced and laughed for seven days and seven nights. They may be dancing even now.

Prince Rose

Once upon a time in the land beyond the seven seas, there lived a king and his three handsome sons. The king troubled himself day and night with the same problem – who among his sons should inherit his country? In order to maintain the unity of his kingdom he did not want to divide it into three parts. At first he thought he would leave it to his eldest son in accordance with justice. But by the next day he had already changed his mind and begun to think that it was best left with his youngest son, Prince Rose, who was his favourite. However, the following day he decided that wouldn't be fair and so he would leave it to his middle son. He pondered over this question without any conclusion for a very long time.

One day the Dog-Headed King invaded and came to occupy his country. The king was killed in the terrible war and the three young princes just barely survived. Nothing was left but their swords and their rifles and their dogs. They did not want to remain as strangers in their own country so they decided to go out into the world. By nightfall the princes arrived at a thick forest. In the middle of it they found a mountain and climbed to the top. There they decided to depart from each other and to try their luck.

Before they departed, they tied a white kerchief to the top of a tree and agreed that they would come back from even the greatest distance to see whether the kerchief had turned red. Red meant that one of the brothers was in trouble. They gave their word of honour that they would come for each other and then said good-bye. The eldest and middle princes went off towards the east and Prince Rose went west.

Prince Rose went through the thick forest and when he reached a meadow at the border of the forest, he found a beautiful diamond palace which stood on a rooster's leg and twirled around continuously! He was very tired and very hungry and thought that he would ask for a night of accommodation and some food at the palace. But how could he stop the palace from revolving? While he thought about this, he put one of his hands into his pocket and found a golden coin there. On it was the sign of a rooster! At once he threw the coin between the rooster's legs and the palace stopped whirling immediately.

Prince Rose walked into the palace's courtyard but he could not see a living soul. As though in a dream, he walked dazedly through the palace, finding no sign of life. Then through a pair of huge oak doors he found a beautifully laid table full of steam-

137

ing foods and wine. Well! He didn't hesitate for even a second before sitting down and beginning to eat and drink heartily. When he was finished he lay himself down on a very comfortable bed in preparation for a long nap. But he had barely closed his eyes when he heard the front door shut with such a bang that the whole palace trembled. He shot out of the bed and ran to the window. Who do you think he saw there? Seven massive giants! This was their palace and now they had come home for their supper!

'My life is over!' Prince Rose thought and quickly hid himself beneath the bed. The giants thudded into the room and the eldest sneezed an enormous sneeze that sent gobs of spit flying all over the room.

'I smell a human', he said.

'Me too', said another, flaring his nostrils widely.

'Me too', said an extra-big one, raising his head and sniffing the breeze that wafted about the house and through the windows. The youngest giant lay down on the floor and looked under the bed, and let out a terrific shriek,

'Come out from under there!' he thundered to Prince Rose.

Oh, poor Prince Rose. He begged them for his life but completely in vain. As soon as he had rolled himself out from under the bed, the giants tore him into pieces which they threw out of the window. After this, they sat down at the table and ate and drank a lot. After dinner they lay down to sleep and were quiet until the following morning. In the morning they woke up and left for the day.

When the palace's door had closed a snake with the head of a beautiful girl glided out from its hiding place. She collected every piece of Prince Rose and fitted them together and then touched them with a piece of magic grass. Then she sprinkled some water of eternal youth on the body and wonder of wonders! The prince came back to life and he was stronger and more handsome than ever. Meanwhile the beautiful girl-headed snake lost a little bit of her snake-skin which peeled away up to her armpit. And she disappeared as if the earth had swallowed her up.

Prince Rose looked for her everywhere. He wanted to thank her for saving his life. He returned to the palace and thought, 'I feel much stronger now. This time I won't hide under the bed but I will fight the giants.'

He had a delicious supper again and after dinner he leant out of the window of the palace and waited for the giants. It wasn't long before the palace's door shut with a bang and the giants came barreling in. As soon as they stepped into the courtyard they saw Prince Rose staring at them from the window.

'Look!' the eldest cried, 'that little pest is still alive!'

They began throwing rocks and branches at him, and then they ran up and tore him to pieces again and threw his pieces out of the window. But the next morning when the giants left the beautiful girl-headed snake glided out from her hiding place again and pieced the prince back together. She touched him with a magic grass and sprinkled some water of eternal youth on his body. And while she was doing this, her snake skin peeled away down to her waist. Before Prince Rose could thank her for her help the beautiful girl-headed snake once again disappeared as if the earth had swallowed her up.

When Prince Rose came to his senses, he felt even seven times stronger than the previous day and was confident that he could overcome the giants now. 'I am ready to fight with them' he thought. He went to the palace and had supper. After dinner he went back to the courtyard and waited for the giants. It wasn't long before he heard the trembling of their heavy footsteps. The prince waved his arms in the air. 'Over here you louts!' he shouted. 'I drank your wine and now I'll have your blood!'

Oh, the giants laughed and laughed as they surrounded the brave prince. But Prince Rose was a bit too big for his britches. He managed to slash at their clothes and scratch them with his sword, but the giants quickly overcame him and tore him to smithereens.

The following morning was peaceful as the beautiful girl-headed snake appeared once again to fit the prince back together. She touched him with a piece of magic grass and then sprinkled him with some water from the spring of eternal youth. Well, this time, Prince Rose sprang to his feet one hundred times stronger than before. He watched as the girl-headed snake lost all of her snake skin and stood before him in her natural form. Who do you think the prince saw? Why, a very beautiful girl as dazzling as the sun!

'Are you surprised Prince Rose?' But the prince couldn't speak. 'Well anyway, I'm a princess and my father was the king of this country until the giants killed him. My life was saved only by my old nurse who turned me into a snake. However, I no longer need this snake skin because you are strong enough to overcome the giants now.'

And Prince Rose said, 'Our fate is similar, beautiful princess. My father was killed too and my country was lost. But you saved my life three times and I am in your debt! I hope that from now on we will be always together.'

'Dear prince, I wish for the same thing,' the princess said and promptly they fell into each other's arms.

The evening came and the giants arrived along with it. They saw the prince and the princess from a distance and immediately understood what had happened. They vowed that it wouldn't ever happen again.

'Oh, Princely, princely! Come over here princely!' the giants called.

'No, you come over here' said the brave young prince. 'In this direction!'

'Okay, you sure are a smart one, but I will kill you anyway!' the oldest giant said.

'Hurry up, you big dumb giant. I don't have all day!' Prince Rose shouted to him as he pulled out his sword. Next their swords crossed, but the prince had more strength now than one giant. He swung his sword over his head and easily cut off the eldest giant's head...and the second and the third and the fourth and fifth and the sixth giant too. They all shared the first giant's fate.

The princess embraced Prince Rose and they kissed each other and then happily started towards the palace. While they were walking through the courtyard Prince Rose looked in the direction of the mountain where he and his brothers had tied a white kerchief to the top of a tree. A troubled mood immediately overtook him.

'What has happened to you Prince Rose? Your face has changed so much!' the princess was worried.

'Oh, dear god!' said the prince, 'do you see that high mountain?' She nodded. 'There is a bloody red kerchief hanging from a tree at the top. That means that my brothers are in trouble. I must go and help them. I promise that I will return and never depart from you ever again.'

They both cried and then said good-bye. Before Prince Rose left, the princess gave him some magic grass and a jug of the water of eternal youth to use in case his brothers were dead. Travelling day and night, the prince finally arrived at a little house in front of which were two dogs tied up. He recognized them at once. One belonged to his oldest brother and the other belonged to his middle brother. He entered the little house but there didn't appear to be anyone about. Outside he unfastened the dogs and sat down under a tree and made a fire.

'Hmmm' he thought, 'they should be nearby.'

While he sat beside the fire a rabbit ran in his direction. Swiftly he picked up his bow and arrow and shot the rabbit, skinned it and put it on a spit to roast for his dinner. While it was cooking he heard someone begin to talk in the tree above his head.

'I am dying from cold!! I am dying from cold!'

Up in the tree Prince Rose saw a very old and very ugly woman sitting there shivering. 'Well, if you are cold climb down from that tree old woman. Kneel close to my fire and warm yourself up!'

'Oh, no sir, I don't dare. I am afraid of the dogs. They'll tear me to pieces. She rocked slowly on a branch, and then turned her sight to the prince, 'Now you listen carefully son, real carefully. If I throw down a single hair, your throw it into the fire and then, maybe if I'm lucky, the dogs won't hurt me.'

'Fine.' Prince Rose said. 'Throw down that single hair, old woman.'

This old woman was a witch. She threw down a single hair and Prince Rose cast it into the flames. Strangely the dogs became immediately silent and the old woman climbed down from the tree's branches. As soon as her feet reached the ground, she ran into the house and fetched a spit and a frog which she roasted beside the rabbit in the prince's fine fire. Suddenly the old woman threw the frog which was greasy and hot at the prince.

Anger flared up in the prince, he jumped to his feet and pulled out his sword feeling that he could kill the old witch! But as soon as he struck her with his sword, his sword turned into a branch. The old witch jumped to her feet with a wicked laugh and said in her raspy voice,

'Pray, Prince Rose, pray for your life. You killed my seven sons and so I killed your two brothers. Now, I'll kill you too! Ha, ha, ha!'

Prince Rose called out for the dogs but they could not move. In fact he could not move either! Luckily he remembered the water of eternal youth and sprinkled a few drops on the dogs and on himself. The dogs leapt up and bit the witch once. She began bleeding and a drop of her blood fell onto the branch in the prince's hand. And it turned back into a sword again.

'Now, old witch, your life is in my hands. Where have you buried my brothers?'

'Under the third tree,' she said, 'but I beg you for my life.'

'No mercy,' said the prince and cut her head off.

At the third tree he dug like a madman until he found the bodies of his two brothers. Neither body had a head so he kept digging until he had unearthed them as well. He fitted their heads to their bodies, touched them with the princess' magic grass and sprinkled them with a few drops of water of eternal youth. His brothers began to rub their eyes as though just waking up and Prince Rose yelled out in his happiness.

Once they were back in the princess' country, they all cried very much after so much adventure and hard time. A splendid wedding was planned for the following day and Prince Rose became the king of the Giants' country. After the wedding feasts the young king led his army against the enemy of his fathers' country. Victory was theirs! They reoccupied their homeland and King Rose left the home kingdom to his brothers. Everyone lived very happily from then on.

The One-and-Only Prince

Once upon a time, in the land beyond the glass mountains there lived a king named Dalton. He reigned over so many countries that he could not count them all. He believed that he reigned over every country in the world and that he was the only king in existence. This thought comforted him. Although King Dalton's kingdom stretched beyond where the eye could see, he was not happy, as he did not have any sons or daughters.

His sadness grew as time passed. His wife was even unhappier than he. The king and queen did not know what would happen to their many countries when they died from this world. One morning King Dalton and the queen went for a walk in the garden to admire the flowers and trees, when suddenly the queen stopped in the middle of the path and said to her husband,

'Look at this, my dear, it is surely a miracle! A white lily grew out of this thorn-bush and it was not cut by the thorns.'

The king smiled at his wife and took her hand gently. As they were looking at the lily a bird flew out from the thorn-bush. At the bottom of the bush was a nest. Inside were four young birds. When the queen saw them she started crying.

'Even this little bird has four youngsters and I don't have any.'

A fairy must have heard the queen's cry, because when she woke up the next morning, she found a little golden-haired boy in her bed! The sadness in the king's court disappeared and everyone became so happy! King Dalton called together his countries' scholars and ordered them to find a good name for his son.

'Find a name that no one else in the whole wide world has.' The king said.

The wise men sat for many days and nights, they thought and talked about different names and submitted their ideas to the king, but he did not like any of them. One day he left the scholars and went for a walk. While he was walking, he met an old woman who asked him for a little charity, but the king was not in a good mood,

'Don't you see, old beggar, that I have a very big problem?'

'What is the matter Your Majesty, perhaps I can help you?' said the old woman.

'I called together all the country's wise men and they cannot help me, so how do you think you could help me?' The king appeared to be very upset indeed, so the beggar decided to help him.

'Your Majesty, let me talk to your wise men.' The king didn't have any better ideas so he nodded to the woman and together they walked along the path towards the palace.

This beggar woman said to the scholars, 'Our king has only one son and it makes sense that his name should be prince One-and-Only.'

The scholars looked at each other. Slowly smiles crept onto their lips.

'Yes, yes,' said one, 'that sounds like a very good name.'

'The only logical name really!' said another.

And the king also liked this name. 'You have helped me so much, old woman, the prince's name shall be One-and-Only.' And in his joy he gave a satchel of gold and silver to the old woman.

Many years passed and the prince became a young man. He started to wonder whether there were other kingdoms in the world besides his father's.

'My dear father, I think there could be more kingdoms elsewhere. It would be very wise for me to go and learn about the world.'

The king laughed heartily. 'Oh my son, banish such ideas from your mind. Believe me, ours is the only kingdom. I have never heard of any other in all my years. When I die you can have my whole kingdom that is the whole world. Don't worry, nothing will attack us!'

But the prince was not satisfied with his father's answer and while he slept that night he had a dream. He saw an old man who told him, 'If your father thinks there are no other kingdoms besides his, he is wrong. There are many kings in the world and one among them is especially dangerous--he has as many countries in his king-dom as your father. This King's name is Absolon. He has three sons and three daugh-ters. The three sons are ready to attack your father's lands. Go right away to Abso-lon's court. Perhaps you will win Absolon's youngest daughter's hand in marriage. She might be a good match for you.'

The following morning the prince went to his father and repeated the old man's words. 'I have made up my mind, my father. I am leaving right away and I will not know peace until I find King Absolon's court.' His father tried to talk him out of leaving but he could not change his mind. In the end, the king realized that he could not convince him to stay.

'Very well, my son,' he said, 'if you are ready to leave, take my best one thousand soldiers with you for protection.'

'I don't need any soldiers father,' said the prince, 'only my trusted servant, Haba-kuk, will accompany me.'

'Fine. Then at least take gold and silver. I will give you twelve carts full.'

'Oh father, thank you for your kindness, but I will only need a hundred gold pieces.'

'Very well. If you don't need soldiers or gold and silver, only a hundred coins, then take a golden-haired steed from my stallion.'

'I don't need a golden-haired steed, my father. I have my lean filly, I will take him with me and Habakuk will be happy with his old horse.' Prince One-and-Only went to the meadow with his servant Habakuk to find the lean filly and the old horse. In the palace attic they found two old bridles and put them on their horses. In the cellar they found two old saddles, which were at least a hundred years old, and they put those on the horses as well. Prince One-and-Only chose the rustiest sword among them all for his weapon.

When he was ready to leave he went to his mother and father to say good-bye. As soon as the prince and his servant had left the palace the prince's lean filly started to gallop and soon he was running at full speed through the Glass Mountains, valleys and thick forests--like a fast wind. Habakuk followed them as fast as he could on his horse. They rode through three countries in one day.

On the seventh day of their journey they reached a big forest. It was already dark and so they looked for a place to sleep. Prince One-and-Only said 'Look Habakuk, along the path, I can see a light. Let's go, perhaps it is a house where we can stay.'

They started to go in the direction of the light and, indeed, they reached a little house. But as soon as they were near the door a nine-headed dragon-dog appeared and began running towards them. Flames spewed from its throat. It clearly wanted to consume both of them with his flames and their horses too. Prince One-and-Only pulled out his rusty sword and cut off seven of its heads. But the dragon-dog still had his two other heads and he jumped on prince One-and-Only's horse. The prince struck him again and cut off the dog's two remaining heads.

The pair dismounted from their horses and went into the house. There they found an old woman eating her dinner. Her nose reached the ground. They greeted her. 'Good evening, my old lady.'

The old woman replied 'How did you get in here? My dragon-dog kills everyone who dares approach my house.'

Prince One-and-Only did not say what had happened to her dog. The old woman ran out to the courtyard and started calling her dog. Habakuk said, 'Majestic Prince, my sweet master, it would be better if you told her the truth. If this old witch finds out before we tell her, she will try to kill us.' The prince took Habakuk's advice and ran after the old woman.

'You are calling your dog in vain, my dear old lady, I have to confess that he is dead—I cut off all of his heads.'

The old woman stopped calling for her dog and turned towards the prince. 'Well, you can thank God that you told me the truth otherwise you both would have died terrible deaths at my hands. Come along.' The valiant prince and his wise servant followed the old woman into her small house where she cooked them a delicious supper. She asked them about their plans and what it was that they were looking for. Prince One-and-Only told her that they were looking for King Absolon's palace.

'Oh, my dear son' said the old woman, 'I have heard of King Absolon's country but I don't know where you can find it. But go to bed now rest well. In the morning I will show you the way through the seven forests and seven plains. Once you have passed the seventh plain you will reach a black forest. In the middle of this forest lives my sister who is nine hundred years old. She knows every corner of this world and I am sure she will know where King Absolon lives.'

So they stayed for the night and in the morning they departed. They went through the seven forests and seven plains, and reached the black forest where the nine hundred year old woman lived. Indeed her house was in the middle of the darkest forest either man had ever visited. From a distance they saw the light of a candle in a window. But this house was also guarded by a dragon-dog and this dog had twelve heads! When they were quite close to the house, the dragon-dog started to run towards them. He spewed flames from his twelve throats but prince One-and-Only immediately cut off nine of his heads with his sword. The dragon-dog fumbled and ran into the house howling from the terrific pain.

Prince One-and-Only and Habakuk dismounted their horses and knocked on the door. An old woman appeared,

'Good evening my old lady.'

'Good evening, my sons. Tell me, what did you do with my dog? He can kill twelve men at once. How is it that you are alive?' She stared at the prince intently, 'I confess that I cut off nine of his heads,' the prince said. 'Oh, never mind, I can see that you are a brave young man', said the old woman 'but tell me what are you looking for here in the back of the beyond?'

Prince One-and-Only explained that he was looking for the court of King Absolon.

'King Absolon's court? I was there about, oh, five, maybe six hundred years ago, but I could not find it anymore.' She smiled, 'I'm not as young as I used to be. Don't worry, my sweet son, tomorrow morning my servants will arrive. They are the reptiles and the birds of the world. I am sure that they will be able to show you the way.'

They were given a sumptuous dinner and beds to sleep in for the night. Over supper, prince One-and-Only told his story—who he was and why he wanted to find

Absolon's court. The next morning the world's reptiles and birds arrived in the old woman's courtyard and made a terrific ruckus. The prince and his servant could not have slept longer even if they had wanted.

The old woman went out to meet her animals. Prince One-and-Only and Habakuk followed. She asked, 'Who among you have ever been to King Absolon's court?' All were silent. Minutes passed. 'Well have any of you heard of him?' she spoke more insistently.

'We don't know it,' they said, 'but perhaps the lame eagle knows of it although we left him far behind somewhere in the forest.'

'Fine, go and find him. Tell him I want him here immediately.'

The birds and the reptiles went away and before the sun set, the old eagle arrived at the courtyard. He moved slowly as he was lame in his right leg and both of his wings were hanging by his side, sweeping the ground.

'Listen, lame eagle,' said the old woman, 'tell us, if you know the whereabouts of King Absolon and his court?'

The eagle answered, 'Yes, I know. I killed many of his lambs and a soldier shot one of my legs. They write poems with my feathers about King Dalton's country. They certainly plan to attack it.'

'If you know the way to King Absolon's country, go and take prince One-and-Only with you.'

Prince One-and-Only and Habakuk thanked the old woman for her kindness and said good-bye. They set off, following the lame eagle. Seven days and seven nights were spent travelling and they did not rest until they reached the top of the highest mountain. It was so high that their heads nearly touched the stars.

The eagle said, 'Look down prince One-and-Only. At the bottom of this mountain there is the city of King Absolon and in the middle of the city there is his diamond palace. I cannot go any further with you but pull one of my feathers out of my right wing and press it between your fingers. While you are pressing it, three drops of water will drip into your palms. Rub your hands together and say, 'I wish I were where I want to be; and you will be there. Moreover, you will fly like a bird and you can choose whatever bird you wish to be. You can also pull one of my feathers from my left wing and you can use it to write even if you don't have any ink.'

Prince One-and-Only pulled one feather from the lame eagle's right wing and then one from his left wing. And then the eagle said good-bye to him. As the eagle disappeared prince One-and-Only told his servant,

'My dear Habakuk, I want you to stay with the horses and look after them. Don't worry about me, I will be back soon.'

'Fine, my master. I will stay here. Good luck and God be with you.'

They parted and prince One-and-Only took out the feather that had come from the eagle's right wing and, as the eagle suggested, pressed it hard in his hand. Three drops of water fell on his palm and he rubbed his hands together and said, 'I wish I were in king Absolon's court in the form of a white dove.'

He had hardly finished saying those words when he became a white dove. He flapped his wings once or twice and flew to the top of King Absolon's palace. He settled himself high in the rafters of the diamond palace and began to coo. All the people in the court listened to the white dove's cooing and the king himself came down to the courtyard with his three daughters. The princesses would have given anything to catch the dove. The king wanted his daughters to be happy so he asked for one of his best hunters and said to him, 'Shoot this dove but be careful not to kill him.' The hunter shot once, twice and a third time but the dove always managed to fly away just in time.

'He will come down if we bring him some grains of wheat to eat,' said the princesses. And they ran back to the palace and brought some grains of wheat. They placed the grains on the ground and beckoned to the dove, 'Come down, come down beautiful white dove!"

And that is what happened. The dove suddenly flew down from the palace's rafters and started to pick at the grains of wheat. The eldest princess tried to catch him, but as soon as she was near, the dove flew away. And then the middle princess tried to catch him but he flew away from her, too. And then the little princess whispered to him,

'Come here, my beautiful white dove!'

And the dove flew straight onto the right arm of the little princess and started to coo softly.

Oh, you can imagine the princesses' happiness! They picked up the white dove and took him to the palace in a golden cage. But as soon as they hung the cage upon the wall in the king's room, the white dove became silent. They gave him some seeds and water but he did not eat and did not drink. He bowed his head and seemed very sad.

One day, and then two days, passed but the white dove's mood did not change. The following night the little princess had a dream. In her dream someone told her that she should bring the cage into her room. As soon as she woke up she went to her father and told him of her dream. The king said, 'Of course you can take the cage to your room, my sweet daughter.' And the princess did just that. She placed it on her golden table and at that moment the dove once again started to coo. He cooed the

whole day! In the evening the little princess left the dove alone and went to have her supper with her family. After supper everybody went back to his or her rooms, including the little princess.

How surprised she was when she entered her room! Everything was covered in a bright light from prince One-and-Only's clothing. It shone brightly as the prince stood before her in his human form!

'Don't be scared, beautiful princess, I am Prince One-and-Only.' He said. 'I am the son of King Dalton and I came here in disguise as a white dove. I heard that your brothers are planning to take away my father's lands.'

'Oh my goodness,' said the little princess, 'you're right. My brothers hatched that plan a long time ago.'

'I don't mind if they come because I am not afraid of them.' The prince said. 'I only think of you, my beautiful princess. Will you come back with me?'

And the youngest princess did not think for even a moment, 'I would go with you even to the end of the world, Prince One-and-Only, but how could we get away from this palace when every door is guarded by two men?'

Of course this was not a problem for the prince. He took one of the lame eagle's feathers from his pocket and showed it to the princess, 'Look here, if we rub three drops of water from this feather into our palms then it will take us anywhere we want to go.'

'That is wonderful,' said the princess, 'but before we leave I would like to write a note to my father and tell him where we are going.'

'Fine,' the prince said, 'I have another feather, you can use it to write with.' After the princess finished writing the letter to her father they took the feather and dropped three drops of water onto their palms and rubbed them into their hands. And the prince said, 'I wish we were on the top of the mountain where my servant is waiting for us.' He envisioned both of them as white doves and everything happened just as he had wished. They turned into white doves and by dawn they were on the top of the mountain. Once back into human form, the prince, the princess and Habakuk mounted their horses and they started to make their way home.

They did not get far when they heard someone following them. The princess turned to see who it was and she got very scared. 'Oh my god! My eldest brother is coming! Your life is in danger, my dear One-and-Only!' At that moment the eldest son of king Absolon arrived beside them and pulled out his sword. Prince One-and-Only pulled out his sword too and he hit the prince with a single stroke. The prince fell to the ground.

The princess' brother stood up with great difficulty, mounted his horse and galloped away to his father's kingdom. Once he had returned, he said to his father, 'Well I am afraid we cannot conquer King Dalton's lands. It seems Prince One-and-Only is much stronger than me.'

'We will see if he is stronger than me,' cried out the brave middle son and he galloped after Prince One-and-Only.

As it turned out the same fate befell him that had befallen his older brother. And the youngest prince fared no better.

Having beaten the three brothers there were no other obstacles for Prince One-and-Only to overcome. He rode home with his princess. At home the king and the queen were jubilant to see him with his bride as they thought they would never see him again. Of course they had a wonderful wedding and the young couple lived happily ever after.

The Young Shepherd and the Wolf

Once upon a time, a very long time ago, far beyond the end of the world at the border of a forest, there lived once a young shepherd. One evening when he had already gone to bed a big wolf came knocking at his door,

'Young shepherd open your door a little wider'

'No, I won't, because you will eat me.'

'Do not be afraid, young shepherd, I only want to warm myself up.'

The young shepherd opened the door a little and the wolf's head appeared in the opening. And he asked the young shepherd again,

'Young shepherd let the rest of me come inside too.'

'No, I don't dare because you're going to eat me.'

'Do not be afraid, young shepherd, I only want to warm myself up a bit.'

So the young shepherd opened a door a bit more and let the wolf's body come into the room.

'How nice and warm it is here,' said the wolf. 'Won't you let my tail to come inside too, young shepherd? It also needs some warmth.'

The young shepherd thought about it. The wolf's head and back were already in the room and he felt sorry for him, so he decided to give the wolf a chance and let his tail come in. This was how that the wolf's whole body came to be in the room. And the wolf sat down beside the stove and said,

'Young shepherd, how about some bread and sausage?'

The young shepherd gave him some bread and sausage and the wolf fell asleep after this good supper and while he lay sleeping the young shepherd changed his mind,

'If the wolf wakes up he is going to eat me' he was thinking very fast. He quickly put a big pot of water on his stove's top to boil. Once it began boiling, he took the pot outside of the house and poured the boiling water through the window over the sleeping wolf. Oh! The wolf howled in pain as the boiling water seared the hair from his head. The young shepherd climbed a tall tree to watch what would happen next.

The bald wolf ran out of the house howling and his howls brought together all of the wolves in the forest. About one hundred silver-furred animals loyally gathered together when they heard their brother's anguish. They snapped their teeth when they saw the young shepherd up in the tree and then they began making so much noise that he began to shake. And the wolves all went under the tall tree where the young shepherd was hiding and stood on each other's backs to try and reach him. But the one hundred wolves could not reach the young shepherd. They began howling again and three other wolves ran from the forest to join them. One hundred and three wolves! And the three newly arrived wolves climbed up to the hundredth wolf's back. Now the young shepherd was within reach.

You can imagine how frightened the young shepherd became! He thought that his life was over! So he started to yell,

'Boiling water for the bald wolf! Boiling water for the bald wolf!'

Oh my God! The bald wolf became extremely scared and he jumped out under the hundred and three wolves and ran away like the devil. As the bald wolf jumped out, the hundred and three wolves all fell to the ground and broke their necks.

Then the young shepherd pulled off the wolves' skins and sold them for a lot of money at the city fair. He definitely lived happily ever after.

The Lily Palko

There was once a king in the White Kingdom who had a son who was as small as a bean. His name was Palko. For many days and nights the king worried about what would happen to his son if he, himself, should die. He imagined that the neighbouring kings would take away his kingdom as his tiny son could not possibly protect it. The queen worried even more, she cried for many days and nights and became very sick from so much crying. The king consulted the best doctors but none of them could cure her. When the queen felt that her last hour was near she asked for her husband,

'My dear husband, when I die please bury me in the garden, plant a single lily on my grave and hire some guards to protect it. If someone were to steal that lily I would not rest peacefully.' Soon after the queen died. The king cried many tears for his queen and his sadness cut him to his core. After the funeral he announced to the whole country that whoever had lilies should bring them to his court and the most beautiful one would be planted on the queen's grave.

People brought lilies from all corners of the kingdom. There were so many of them that there wasn't any space left in the courtyard. The question on everyone's mind was, which one was the most beautiful? Seventy-seven gardeners sorted them for seven days and seven nights but they could not agree. Every one of them had a favourite and the pressure to choose a single lily became so great that they started to fight with each other.

A large commotion ensued and the king ran out of his palace and asked what was going on. The seventy-seven gardeners answered all at the same time:

'Your Majesty, the others refuse to accept that the lily I chose is the most beautiful one among them all.'

'Your Majesty, choosing a lily for a deceased queen requires a sensitive and finely-tuned nature like mine.' Said one of the gardeners.

'Your Majesty, I have the expertise and skill necessary to hand-pick a high quality lily.' Said yet another. There were many other voices wishing to be heard as well. The king was unsure how to resolve the disagreements. He had to think for a minute. Finally he had an idea and he called his son, Palko.

'Come little 'bean', why don't you close your eyes and select one of these seventy-seven lilies.' Palko felt hurt that his father had called him a 'bean', but he did as he was told. Closing his eyes he reached out his hand and selected an especially

154

lovely flower. As soon as he made his selection, the king asked the people, 'Who brought this lily?'

An old woman, whose nose was so long it reached her knees, came forward from the crowd and said,

'Your Majesty, I offer my life to you. I brought this lily from Ilona, the fairies' queen's garden.' The king was startled, but unsure whether to believe this strange old woman. While he held the lily, its petals turned into bright, white diamonds. The king was nearly blinded from the lily's bright light!

'Now I indeed believe you,' the king said smiling, 'this lily really is from the garden of the fairies' queen. You, old woman, will stay in my palace and will plant this lily and look after it.' The woman nodded and knelt down before him for it was an honour to live in the king's palace. But the king was also a harsh ruler and he continued, 'But if someone steals the lily I will chop your head off!'

'Very well your Majesty,' said the old woman, trembling a little. 'I will plant it and take good care of it.' She then rose to her feet and said, 'But Your Majesty, I ask for only one thing, please let Prince Palko stay with me to guard the lily every night.'

'That is fine with me,' said the king, 'I do not have any use for him. But listen, little 'bean', I will chop your head off too if even a single petal of this lily is stolen.'

The old woman planted the flower and stayed there, guarding it. When the evening arrived Palko put a small loaf of bread in his satchel and placed its thin strap round his neck and walked down to the garden. The old woman was sitting beside the lily spinning some yarn.

'It is good to see you,' she said to Palko, 'I am already sleepy so I am going to lie down but when the clock strikes midnight, you must wake me up because exactly at that time the fairies' queen will come and if we are not awake she will take the lily back to her garden.'

The old woman lay down to sleep and Palko kept guard. He took the loaf of bread from his satchel, tore off a piece and started to eat. Suddenly a dwarf appeared in front of him. He was even smaller than Palko and he had a beard that was seven yards long.

'Good evening, Palko,' said the dwarf.

'Good evening,' said Palko between two bites of bread, 'Are you looking for anything?'

'I will tell you soon enough.' the dwarf said. 'Do you know who it is that you are watching over?' Palko shook his head, his eyes wide. The dwarf rubbed his hands together and leaned closer, his voice a little lower, 'She is the daughter of the dwarf king

but is disguised as a lily. I'll tell you her story.' He said this while his eyes were lighting up. Palko put down the piece of bread that he was eating and the dwarf cleared his voice and began:

'Ilona, the fairies' queen visited the country of the dwarfs some time ago and there she saw the princess who was as beautiful as the brightest star in the sky. The fairies' queen begged the dwarfs' king to let his daughter come to her palace for a visit. She told the king that the princess would become even more beautiful if she could stay with her for a while. The fairy begged and begged until the king finally let his daughter go with her. Alas, the king has not seen her since. The fairies' queen became very jealous of the dwarf-princess' beauty and she treated her so wickedly that the princess died in sorrow. The princess' old nurse, who went with her from her father's court, spent her time crying beside the princess' grave. But, suddenly a diamond lily grew from the grave and the lily started to talk to the old woman. The voice said, 'Do not cry, my sweet nurse, just pull me out of the ground. I am your princess. I had a dream last night that the queen of the White Kingdom was dying and she asked that a lily be planted on her grave. Take me there and plant me on her grave because my dream also told me I cannot re-appear as a princess until I fulfill her wish.'

'Oh, you cannot imagine how happy the old woman was!' continued the dwarf, 'She pulled the lily from the ground and took it to the White Kingdom, right here, to your father's palace. However there was a witch at Ilona, the fairies' queen's palace who overheard this conversation between the old woman and the lily and she revealed everything to the queen. You can be sure that the queen will not find her peace until she steals this lily from your mother's grave. Take good care of this lily, Palko and you will be rewarded!'

As he said these words, the dwarf put his seven-yard long beard between his legs and flew away on it so quickly that Palko had no time to blink. 'Well,' thought Palko, 'It was a strange story. I will have to be even more cautious.' Palko became lost in his thoughts when he suddenly heard some loud rumbling above his head as if thousands and thousands of birds were flying over him.

Before he had a chance to look around, twelve fairies appeared before him. Wearing bright golden dresses they surrounded Palko, twirling and leaping in the air. And their singing was so beautiful that it seemed as though angels had descended upon earth. They asked Palko to go with them,

'You had better come with us,' they said, 'We'll have to take you away with the lily anyway whether you want it or not.'

'How can you imagine that I would ever go with you?' shouted Palko, 'Get out of here immediately, all of you, or you will lose your lives!' And he shook the old woman, 'Wake up, old woman, we have some intruders and they have come for the lily!' The old woman woke up immediately and started to shout at the fairies,

'Have you no shame? How dare you bother this innocent soul, you cruel creatures! Wait until I take care of you!' She picked up her spinning wheel and beat the fairies with it. They moaned and groaned and flew away, back to their queen. You can imagine how angry their queen became! She scolded them for not being able to trick an old woman and a young lad.

The following night the fairies' queen sent another twelve fairies. But on that night Palko took his sword with him and used it scare them away.

Finally Ilona, the fairies' queen decided that she would have to steal the lily away herself.

The next evening the old woman was asleep and Palko was on guard when suddenly someone was calling him. He looked everywhere but could not see anyone. And then, from nowhere, there was a voice, 'Look at me here,' it said, 'I am the lily, daughter of the king of the dwarfs.'

As she said this, the lily turned back into a splendidly beautiful princess. Oh, Palko became so happy! He nearly began dancing in his joy. The fairies' queen can come now, he thought, she definitely won't find the lily. The princess could tell what Palko was thinking. She told him, 'Palko, you should know the queen will return for me soon, even though I have turned back into a princess. She'll take me away if she finds me here. But if my butterfly-coach were here, I would be home safely in my father's palace in a flash!'

As the princess took a deep breath, the dark night turned bright, and wonder of wonders! A golden coach pulled by two shimmering butterflies descended from the air. Many dwarfs surrounded the coach, some with wings, others flying on the backs of butterflies and others tumbling head over heals in their joy at having found their princess.

'Now, Palko,' asked the princess, 'Are you coming with me?' Palko nodded and jumped into the coach. And the butterflies flew away with them. When they reached the clouds the princess asked Palko, 'Look down Palko, what do you see?'

'It looks like a monster spitting flames toward us.'

'That is the fairies' queen's seven-legged horse.' said the princess, 'If we can reach the place between the sun and the moon then we're safe because the seven-legged horse cannot fly that high.' The butterflies fluttered along with the coach as fast as they could but they were growing tired. 'Now what do you see?' asked the princess again.

'I fear that the fairies' queen will reach us in a second.' As soon as Palko said this he felt the queen's horse's flame on his back.

'Hurry up, as fast as you can my sweet butterflies,' shouted the princess her butterflies. They made a valiant effort even as fire singed the back wheel of the coach. Then suddenly the sky seemed to open up and stars twinkled everywhere and the fire could not reach them anymore. They had flown above the moon! The fairies' queen became furious as she watched Palko and the princess escape into the top of the sky. Palko and the princess flew higher and higher up between the sun and the moon. Suddenly Palko said,

'Oh my goodness my dear princess, we forgot the old woman on the ground!'

'Oh!' the princess clapped her hands in shock, 'you're right...we did forget her, and now the queen will take her back to her palace and kill her.' The poor princess cried for her old nurse as she thought she would never see her again. Palko tried to console her.

'Don't worry, I will bring her back, but first we should go to your father's country.' And the princess smiled through her tears at Palko. With luck on their side they arrived at the dwarf king's palace. The old king was elated to see his daughter again and he happily greeted Palko saying that he could not think of a more suitable son-in-law! He immediately handed the young prince half of his kingdom and his daughter's hand in marriage.

But the princess announced that she would not have her wedding dance if her old nurse were not there. Hearing this, Palko became anxious. He knew that it would not be easy to rescue the old woman from the fairies' queen's palace that was guarded by hundreds of fairies. But then the dwarf with a seven-yard long beard appeared in front of him.

'Why are you so sad when you should be very happy?' he asked Palko. And Palko told him about the princess' wish for him to rescue the old woman. 'Oh don't worry about that. Leave it to me!' said the dwarf. 'I'll fly to the fairies' queen's court. Once I'm there I'll pick up the old woman and fly back with her.'

As soon as he said this, he put his beard between his two legs and disappeared as though the air had swallowed him up. He arrived at Ilona, the fairies' queen's court at just the right time. He told the old woman to sit on his beard and instantly they disappeared. The queen tried to saddle her seven-legged horse to catch them but her horse had broken its seventh leg that very day and could not move.

And the dwarf arrived safely with the old woman at the king's palace. Now there was happiness everywhere! Palko and the princess had a splendid wedding. Palko made the dwarf his prime minister and the young king and his bride still live happily even to this day.

Printed in Hungary